PRAISE FOR *Monica Wood*

"The loving character portraits that form her stories help us understand…the human condition."
—*The Boston Globe*

"Piercingly beautiful . . . Intelligent and warmhearted."
—*Cleveland Plain Dealer*

"These quirky stories reaffirm faith in human resilience."
—*Booklist*

"Wood's stories [are] filled with light and hope."
—*Titan*

"Wood reveals joyousness in the confounding complexity of humanity."
—*Stylist* (UK)

ALSO BY MONICA WOOD

ERNIE'S ARK

ERNIE'S ARK

THE
✤ ABBOTT FALLS ✤
STORIES

Monica Wood

David R. Godine, Publisher
BOSTON

Published in 2020 by
DAVID R. GODINE, PUBLISHER, INC.
Boston, Massachusetts
www.godine.com

First published in a slightly different version in hardcover by
Chronicle Books, San Francisco in 2002 and in softcover by
Ballantine Books, New York in 2003.

LIBRARY OF CONGRESS CATALOGING-IN-PUBLICATION DATA

Names: Wood, Monica, author.
Title: Ernie's ark : the Abbott Falls stories / Monica Wood.
Identifiers: LCCN 2020019413 | ISBN 9781567926910 (hardcover) |
ISBN 9781567926682 (paperback) | ISBN 9781567926743 (ebook)
Subjects: LCSH: Maine—Social life and customs—Fiction. |
Community Life—Fiction.
Classification: LCC PS3573.O5948 E76 2020 | DDC 813/.54--dc23
LC record available at https://lccn.loc.gov/2020019413

FIRST PRINTING, 2020
Printed in Canada

for Cathe, who remembers everything,
and in loving memory of our parents

CONTENTS

Ernie's Ark

ERNIE WHITTEN, *pipefitter*

Ernie was an angry man. He felt his anger as something apart from him, like an urn of water balanced on his head, a precarious weight that affected his gait, the set of his shoulders, his willingness to move through a crowd. He was angry at the melon-faced CEO from New York City who had forced a strike in a paper mill all the way up in Maine—a decision made, Ernie was sure, in that fancy restaurant atop the World Trade Center where Ernie had taken his wife, Marie, for their forty-fifth wedding anniversary last winter, another season, another life. Every Thursday as he stood in line at Manpower Services to wait for his unemployment check he thought of that jelly-assed CEO—Henry John McCoy, with his parted blond hair—yucking it up at a table laid out in bleached linen and phony silver, figuring out all the ways he could cut a man off at the knees three weeks before retirement.

Oh, yes, he was angry. At the deadbeats and no-accounts who stood in line with him: the Davis boy, who couldn't look a man in the eye; the Shelton girl, with hair dyed so bright you could light a match on her ponytail. There were others in line—millwrights and tinsmiths and machine tenders whose years and labor had added up to a puff of air—but he couldn't bear to look at them, so he reserved his livid stare for the people in line who least resembled himself.

He was angry at the kids from Broad Street who cut through his yard on their dirt bikes day after day, leaving moats of mud through the flowery back lawn Marie had sprinkled a season ago with Meadow-in-a-Can. He was angry with the police department, who didn't give a hoot about Marie's wrecked grass. He'd even tried city hall, where an overpaid blowhard, whose uncle had worked beside Ernie nineteen years ago on the Number Five, had all but laughed in his face.

When he arrived at the hospital after collecting his weekly check, Marie was being bathed by a teenaged orderly. He had seen his wife in all manner of undress over the years, yet it filled him with shame to observe the yellow hospital sponge applied to her diminishing body by a uniformed kid who was younger than their only grandchild. He went to the lobby to wait, picking up a newspaper from among the litter of magazines.

It was some sort of city weekly, filled with mean political cartoons and smug picture captions fashioned to embarrass the President, but it had a separate section on the arts, Marie's favorite subject. She had dozens of coffee-table books stowed in her sewing room, and their house was filled with framed prints of strange objects—

melted watches and spent shoelaces and sad, deserted diners—that he never liked but had nonetheless come to think of as old friends. He had never known her to miss a Community Concert or an exhibit at the library where she had worked three days a week since she was eighteen; every Sunday of their married life, Ernie had brought in the paper, laid it on the kitchen table, and fished out the arts section to put next to Marie's coffee cup.

The weekly was printed on dirty newsprint—paper from out of state, he surmised. He scanned the cheap, see-through pages, fixing on an announcement for an installation competition, whatever that was. The winning entry would be displayed to the public at the college. Pictured was last year's winner, a tangle of pipes and sheet metal that looked as if somebody had hauled a miniature version of the Number Five machine out of the mill, twisted it into a thousand ugly pieces, then left it to weather through five hundred hailstorms. Not that it would matter now if somebody did. *The Burden of Life*, this installation was called, by an artist who most likely hadn't yet moved out of his parents' house. He thought Marie would like it, though—she had always been a woman who understood people's intentions—so he removed the picture with his jackknife and tucked it into his shirt pocket. Then he faltered his way back up the hall and into her room, where she was sitting up, weak and clean.

"What's the latest?" she asked him.

He sat down on her bleach-smelling bed. She herself smelled of lilac. "McCoy's threatening to fold up shop."

"Sell it, you mean?" She blinked at him. "Sell the mill?"

"That's the rumor."

She put her fragile, ghostly hand on his. "It's been eight months, Ernie. How long can a strike last?" She was thinking, of course, of his pension held hostage, the bills she was racking up.

"We'll be all right," he said. The word *we* always calmed him. He showed her the clipping. "Can you feature this?"

She smiled. "*The Burden of Life*?"

"He should've called it *The Burden of My Big Head*."

She laughed, and he was glad, and his day took the tiniest turn. "Philistine," she said. "You always were such a philistine, Ernie." She often referred to him in the past tense, as if he were the one departing.

That night, after the long drive home, he hung the clipping on the refrigerator before taking Pumpkin Pie, Marie's doddering Yorkshire terrier, for its evening walk. He often waited until nightfall for this walk, so mortified was he to drag this silly-name pushbroom of an animal at the end of a thin red leash. The dog walked with prissy little steps on pinkish feet that resembled ballerina slippers. He had observed so many men just like himself over the years, men in retirement walking wee, quivery dogs over the streets of their neighborhood, a wrinkled plastic bag in their free hand; they might as well have been holding a sign above their heads: Widower.

The night was eerie and silent. FOR SALE signs had popped up even in this neighborhood of old people. This small, good place, once drenched with ordinary hopes and decent money, was beginning to furl like an autumn leaf. At the foot of the downhill slope of Randall Street, Ernie could see the belching smokestacks of Atlantic Pulp & Paper, the dove-gray plume curling up from the valley, an upward, omnipresent cloud rising like a smoke signal, an offering to God. Cancer Valley, a news reporter once called the city of Abbott Falls, but they needed the steam, the smoke, the rising cloud, the heaps and heaps of wood stacked in the railyard, even the smell—the smell of money, Ernie called it—they needed it. He thought of the son of a bitch working his very spot, this very night, wiping the greasy heat from his forehead; he wondered which of life's cruelties had converged upon this man to impel him to cross a picket line, step over a man with a dying wife, and steal his job. Did he, too, have a dying wife? Eight months ago, watching the first of them marching in there under police guard, he could not have mustered a human feeling for the stranger hooking up chlorine cars or running pipe in the bleachery. Ernie's own circumstances, his own livelihood, seemed to melt further into dream every day. Every few weeks there was word of negotiation—another fancy-restaurant meeting between McCoy's boys and the national union—but Ernie held little hope of recovering the bulk of his pension. That, too, felt like knowledge found in a dream.

As he turned up his front walk, he caught the kids from Broad Street crashing again through his property, this time roaring away so fast he could hear a faint shudder from the backyard trees. "Sonsabitches!" he hollered, shaking his fist like the mean old man in the movies. He stampeded into the backyard, where Marie's two apple trees, brittle and untrained, sprouted from the earth in such rootlike twists that they seemed to have been planted upside down. He scanned the weedy lawn, dotted with exhausted clumps of Marie's wildflowers and the first of the fallen leaves, and saw blowdown everywhere, spindly parts of branches scattered like bodies on a battlefield. Planted when their son was born, the trees had never yielded a single decent apple, and now they were being systematically mutilated by a pack of ill-bred boys. He picked up a branch and a few sticks, and by the time he reached his kitchen he was weeping, pounding his fist on the table, cursing a God who would let a woman like Marie, a big-boned girl who was sweetness itself, wither beneath the death-white sheets of Western Maine General, thirty-eight miles from home.

He sat in the kitchen deep into evening. The dog curled up on Marie's chair and snored. Ernie remembered Marie's laughter from the afternoon and tried to harness it, hear it anew, make it last. The sticks lay sprawled and messy on the table in front of him, their leaves stalled halfway between greenery and dust. All of a sudden— and, oh, it was sweet!—Ernie had an artistic inspiration. He stood up with the shock of it, for he was not an artistic man. The sticks, put together at just the right angle, resembled the hull of a boat. He turned them one way, then another, admiring his idea, wishing Marie were here to witness it.

Snapping on the floodlights, he jaunted into the backyard to collect the remaining sticks, hauling them into the house a bouquet at a time. He took the clipping down from the fridge and studied the photograph, trying to get a sense of scale and size. Gathering the sticks, he descended the stairs to the cellar, where he spent most of the night twining sticks and branches with electrical wire. The dog sat at attention, its wet eyes fixed on Ernie's work. By morning the installation was finished. It was the most beautiful thing Ernie had ever seen.

The college was only four blocks from the hospital, but Ernie had trouble navigating the maze of one-way roads on campus, and found the art department only by following the directions of a frightening girl whose tender lips had been pierced with small gold rings. By the time he entered the lavender art office, he was sweating, hugging his beautiful boat to his chest.

"Excuse me?" said a young man at the desk. This one had a hoop through each eyebrow.

"My installation," Ernie said, placing it on the desk. "For the competition." He presented the newspaper clipping like an admission ticket.

"Uh, I don't think so."

"Am I early?" Ernie asked, feeling foolish. The deadline was six weeks away; he hadn't the foggiest idea how these things were supposed to go.

"This isn't an installation," the boy said, flickering his gaze over the boat. "It's—well, I don't know what it is, but it's not an installation."

"It's a boat," Ernie said. "A boat filled with leaves."

"Are you in Elderhostel?" the boy asked. "They're upstairs, fifth floor."

"I want to enter the contest," Ernie said. And by God,

he did; he had never won so much as a cake raffle in his life, and didn't like one bit the pileup of things he appeared to be losing.

"I like your boat," said a girl stacking books in a corner. "But he's right, it's not an installation." She spread her arms and smiled. "Installations are big."

Ernie turned to face her, a freckled redhead. She reminded him of his granddaughter, who was somewhere in Alaska sharing her medicine cabinet with an unemployed guitar player. "Let me see," the girl said, plucking the clipping from his hand. "Oh, okay. You're talking about the Corthell Competition. This is more of a professional thing."

"Professional?"

"I myself wouldn't *dream* of entering, okay?" offered the boy, who rocked backed in his chair, arms folded like a CEO's. "All the entries come through this office, and most of them are awesome. Museum quality." He made a small, self-congratulating gesture with his hand. "We see the entries even before the judges do."

"One of my professors won last year," the girl said, pointing out the window. "See?"

Ernie looked. There it was, huge in real life—nearly as big as the actual Number Five, in fact, a heap of junk flung without a thought into the middle of a campus lawn. It did indeed look like a Burden.

"You couldn't tell from the picture," Ernie said, reddening. "In the picture it looked like some sort of tabletop size. Something you might put on top of your TV."

The girl smiled. Ernie could gather her whole face without stumbling over a single gold hoop. He took this as a good sign, and asked, "Let's say I did make something of size. How would I get it over here? Do you do pickups, something of that nature?"

She laughed, but not unkindly. "You don't actually build it unless you win. What you do is write up a proposal with some sketches. Then, if you win, you build it right here, on-site." She shrugged. "The *process* is the whole entire idea of the installation, okay? The whole entire community learns from witnessing the *process*."

In this office, where *process* was clearly the most important word in the English language, not counting *okay*, Ernie felt suddenly small. "Is that so," he said, wondering who learned what from the heap of tin Professor Life-Burden had processed onto the lawn.

"Oh, wait, one year a guy *did* build off-site," said the boy, ever eager to correct the world's misperceptions. "Remember that guy?"

"Yeah," the girl said. She turned to Ernie brightly. "One year a guy put his whole installation together at his studio and sent photographs. He didn't win, but the winner got pneumonia or something and couldn't follow through, and this guy was runner-up, so he trucked it here in a U-Haul."

"It was a totem," the boy said solemnly. "With a whole mess of wire things sticking out of it."

"I was a freshman," the girl said by way of an explanation Ernie couldn't begin to fathom. He missed Marie intensely, as if she were already gone.

Ernie peered through the window, hunting for the totem.

"Kappa Delts trashed it last Homecoming," the girl

said. "Those animals have no respect for art." She handed back the clipping. "So, anyway, that really wasn't so stupid after all, what you said."

"Well," said the boy, "good luck, okay?"

As Ernie bumbled out the door, the girl called after him, "It's a cute boat, though. I like it."

At the hospital he set the boat on Marie's windowsill, explaining his morning. "Oh, Ernie," Marie crooned. "You old—you old surprise, you."

"They wouldn't take it," he said. "It's not big enough. You have to write the thing up, and make sketches and whatnot."

"So why don't you?"

"Why don't I what?"

"Make sketches and whatnot."

"Hah! I'd make it for real. Nobody does anything real anymore. I'd pack it into the back of my truck and haul it there myself. A guy did that once."

"Then make it for real."

"I don't have enough branches."

"Then use something else."

"I just might."

"Then do it." She was smiling madly now, fully engaged in their old, intimate arguing, and her eyes made bright blue sparks from her papery face. He knew her well, he realized, and saw what she was thinking: Ernie, there is some life left after everything seems to be gone. Really, there is. And that he could see this, just a little, and that she could see him seeing it, buoyed him. He thought he might even detect some pink fading into her cheeks.

He stayed through lunch, and was set to stay for supper until Marie remembered her dog and made him go home. As he turned from her bed, she said, "Wait. I want my ark." She lifted her finger to the windowsill, where the boat glistened in the filmy city light. And he saw that she was right: it *was* an ark, high and round and jammed with hope. He placed it in her arms and left it there, hoping it might sweeten her dreams.

When he reached his driveway he found fresh tire tracks, rutted by an afternoon rain, running in a rude diagonal from the back of the house across the front yard. He sat in the truck for a few minutes, counting the seconds of his rage, watching the dog's jangly shadow in the dining-room window. He counted to two hundred, checked his watch, then hauled himself out to fetch the dog. He set the dog on the seat next to him—in a different life it would have been a doberman named Rex—and gave it a kiss on its wiry head. "That's from her," he said, and then drove straight to the lumberyard.

ERNIE FIGURED that Noah himself was a man of the soil and probably didn't know spit about boatbuilding. In fact, Ernie's experience in general—forty years of tending machinery, fixing industrial pipe the size of tree trunks, assembling Christmas toys for his son, remodeling bathrooms, building bird boxes and planters and finally, attached dramatically to the side of the house, a sunporch to please Marie—probably had Noah's beat in about a dozen ways. He figured he had the will and enough good tools to make a stab at a decent ark, and he was right: in a week's time he'd completed most of a hull beneath a makeshift staging that covered most of the ground between Marie's sunporch and the neighbor's fence. It was not a hull he would care to float, but he thought of it as a decent artistic representation of a hull; and even more important, it was big enough to qualify as an installation, if he had the guidelines right. He covered the hull with the bargain-priced tongue-and-groove boards he picked up at the lumberyard, leftover four-footers with lots of knots. Every day he worked from sunup to noon, then drove to the hospital to report his progress. Marie listened with her head inclined, her whispery hair tucked behind her ears. She still asked about the strike, but he had little news on that score, staying clean away from the union hall and the picket lines. He had even stopped getting the paper.

Often he turned on the floodlights in the evenings and worked in the cold till midnight or one. Working in the open air, without the iron skull of the mill over his head, made him feel like a newly sprung prisoner. He let the dog patter around and around the growing apparition, and sometimes he even chuckled at the animal's apparent capacity for wonder. The hateful boys from Broad Street loitered with their bikes at the back of the yard, and as the thing grew in size they more often than not opted for the long way round.

At eleven o'clock in the morning on the second day of the second week, a youngish man pulled up in a city car. He ambled down the walk and into the side yard, a clipboard and notebook clutched under one arm. The dog cowered at the base of one of the trees, its dime-sized eyes blackened with fear.

"You Mr. Ernest Whitten?" the man asked Ernie.

Ernie put down his hammer and climbed down from the deck by way of a gangplank that he had constructed in a late-night fit of creativity.

"I'm Dan Little, from the city," the man said, extending his hand.

"Well," Ernie said, astonished. He pumped the man's hand. "It's about time." He looked at the bike tracks, which had healed over for the most part, dried into faint, innocent-looking scars after a string of fine sunny days. "Not that it matters now," Ernie said. "They don't even come through much anymore."

Mr. Little consulted his notebook. "I don't follow," he said.

"Aren't you here about those hoodlums tearing up my wife's yard?"

"I'm from code enforcement."

"Pardon?"

Mr. Little squinted up at the ark. "You need a building permit for this, Mr. Whitten. Plus the city has a twenty-foot setback requirement for any new buildings."

Ernie twisted his face into disbelief, an expression that felt uncomfortably familiar; lately the entire world confused him. "The lot's only fifty feet wide as it is," he protested.

"I realize that, Mr. Whitten." Mr. Little shrugged apologetically. "I'm afraid you're going to have to take it down."

Ernie tipped back his cap to scratch his head. "It isn't a building. It's an installation."

"Say what?"

"An installation. I'm hauling it up to the college when I'm done. Figure I'll have to rent a flatbed or something. It's a little bigger than I counted on."

Mr. Little began to look nervous. "I'm sorry, Mr. Whitten, I still don't follow." He kept glancing back at the car.

"It's an ark," Ernie said, enunciating, although he could see how the ark might be mistaken for a building at this stage. Especially if you weren't really looking, which this man clearly wasn't. "It's an ark," Ernie repeated.

Mr. Little's face took a heavy downward turn. "You're not zoned for arks," he sighed, writing something on the official-pink papers attached to his clipboard.

Ernie glanced at the car. In the driver's seat had appeared a pony-sized yellow Labrador retriever, its quivering nose faced dead forward as if it were planning to set that sucker into gear and take off into the wild blue yonder. "That your dog?" Ernie asked.

Mr. Little nodded.

"Nice dog," Ernie said.

"This one's yours, I take it?" Mr. Little pointed at Marie's dog, who had scutted out from the tree and hidden behind Ernie's pants leg.

"My wife's," Ernie told him. "She's in the hospital."

"I'm sorry to hear that," Mr. Little said. "I'm sure she'll be on the mend in no time."

"Doesn't look like it," Ernie said, wondering why he

didn't just storm the hospital gates, do something sweeping and biblical, stomp through those clean corridors and
defy doctor's orders and pick her up with his bare hands
and bring her home.

Mr. Little scooched down and made clicky sounds at
Marie's dog, who nosed out from behind Ernie's leg to
investigate. "What's his name?" he asked.

"It's, well, it's Pumpkin Pie. My wife named him."

"That's Junie," Mr. Little said, nudging his chin toward the car. "I got her the day I signed my divorce papers. She's a helluva lot more faithful than my wife ever
was."

"I never had problems like that," Ernie said.

Mr. Little got to his feet and shook his head at Ernie's
ark. "Listen, about this, this . . ."

"Ark," Ernie said.

"You're going to have do something, Mr. Whitten.
At the very least, you'll have to go down to city hall,
get a building permit, and then follow the regulations.
Just don't tell them it's a boat. Call it a storage shed or
something."

Ernie tipped back his cap again. "I don't suppose it's
regulation to cart your dog all over kingdom come on city
time."

"Usually she sleeps in the back," Mr. Little said
sheepishly.

"I'll tell you what," Ernie said. "You leave my ark alone
and I'll keep shut about the dog."

Mr. Little looked sad. "Listen," he said, "people can
do what they want as far as I care. But you've got neigh-

bors out here complaining about the floodlights and the noise."

Ernie looked around, half-expecting to see the dirt-bike gang sniggering behind their fists someplace out back. But all he saw were FOR SALE signs yellowing from disuse, and the sagging rooftops of his neighbors' houses, their shades drawn against the sulfurous smell of betrayal.

Mr. Little ripped a sheet off his clipboard and handed it to Ernie. "Look, just consider this a real friendly warning, would you? And just for the record, I hate my job, but I've got bills piling up like everybody else."

Ernie watched him amble back to the car, say something to the dog, who gave her master a walloping with her broad pink tongue. He watched them go, remembering now that he'd seen Mr. Little before, somewhere in the mill—the bleachery maybe, or strolling in the dim recesses near the Number Eight, his face flushed and shiny under his yellow hardhat, clipboard at the ready. Now here he was, trying to stagger his way through the meanwhile, harassing senior citizens on behalf of the city. His dog probably provided him with the only scrap of self-respect he could ferret out in a typical day.

Ernie ran a hand over the rough surface of his ark, remembering that Noah's undertaking had been a result of God's despair. God was sorry he'd messed with any of it, the birds of the air and beasts of the forest and especially the two-legged creatures who insisted on lying and cheating and killing their own brothers. Still, God had found one man, one man and his family, worth saving, and therefore had deemed a pair of everything else worth saving, too. "Come on, dog," he said. "We're going to get your mother."

As happened so often, in so many small, miraculous ways during their forty-five years together, Marie had outthought him. When he got to her room she was fully dressed, her overnight bag perched primly next to her on the bone-white bed, the ark cradled into her lap and tipped on its side. "Ernie," she said, stretching her arms straight out. "Take me home."

He bore her home at twenty-five miles an hour, aware of how every pock in the road rose up to meet her fragile, flesh-wanting spine. He eased her out of the car and carried her over their threshold. He filled all the bird feeders along the sunporch, then took her out to survey the ark. These were her two requests. By morning she looked better. The weather—the warmest fall on record—held. He propped her on a chaise lounge on the sunporch in the brand-new flannel robe their son's wife had sent from California, then wrapped her in a blanket, so that she looked like a benevolent pod person from a solar system ruled by warmth and decency. The dog nestled in her lap, eyes half-closed in ecstasy.

He propped her there so she could watch him work— her third request. And work he did, feeling the way he had when they were first dating and he would remove his shirt to burrow elaborately into the tangled guts of his forest-green 1950 Pontiac. He forgot that he was building the ark for the contest, and how much he wanted to win, and his rage fell like dead leaves from his body as he felt the watchful, sunshiney presence of Marie. He moved one of Marie's feeders to the deck of the ark because she wanted him to know the tame and chittery company of chickadees. The sun shone and shone; the yard did not succumb to the dun colors of fall; the tracks left by the dirt bikes resembled nothing more ominous than the faintest prints left by dancing birds. Ernie unloaded some more lumber, a stack of roofing shingles, a small door. He had three weeks till deadline, and in this strange, blessed season, he meant to make it. .

Marie got better. She sat up, padded around the house a little, ate real food. Several times a day he caught a sharp squeak floating down from the sunporch as she conversed with one of her girlfriends, or with her sister down from Bangor, or with the visiting nurse. He would look up, see her translucent white hand raised toward him—*It's nothing, Ernie, just go back to whatever you were doing*—and recognize the sound after the fact as a strand of her old laughter, high and ecstatic and small-town, like her old self.

"It happens," the nurse told him when he waylaid her on the front walk. "They get a burst of energy toward the end sometimes."

He didn't like this nurse, the way she called Marie "they." He thought of adding her to the list of people and things he'd grown so accustomed to railing against, but because his rage was gone, there was no place to put her. He returned to the ark, climbed onto the deck, and began to nail the last shingles to the shallow pitch of the roof. Marie's voice floated out again, and he looked up again, and her hand rose again, and he nodded again, hoping she could see his smiling, his damp collar, the handsome knot of his forearm. He was wearing the clothes he wore to work back when he was working, a grass-colored gabardine shirt and pants—his greens, Marie called them. In some awful way he recognized this as one of the happiest times of his life; he was brimming with industry and connected to nothing but this one woman, this one patch of earth.

When it was time for Marie's lunch, he climbed down from the deck and wiped his hands on his work pants. Mr. Little was standing a few feet away, a camera raised to his face.

"What's this?" Ernie asked.

Mr. Little lowered the camera. "For our records."

Ernie thought on this for a moment. "I'm willing to venture there's nothing like this in your records."

"Not so far," Mr. Little said. He ducked once, twice, as a pair of chickadees flitted over his head. "Your wife is home, I see."

Ernie glanced over at the sunporch, where Marie lay heavily swaddled on her chaise lounge, watching them curiously. He waved at her, and waited many moments as she struggled to free her hand from the blankets and wave back.

"As long as you've got that camera," Ernie said, "I wonder if you wouldn't do us a favor."

"I'm going to have to fine you, Mr. Whitten. I'm sorry."

"I need a picture of my ark," Ernie said. "Would you do us that favor? All you have to do is snap one extra."

Mr. Little looked around uncertainly. "Sure, all right."

"I'm sending it in to a contest."

"I bet you win."

Ernie nodded. "That's the plan."

Mr. Little helped Ernie dismantle the staging, such as it was, and soon the ark stood alone in the sun, as round and full-skirted as a giant hen nestled on the grass. The chickadees, momentarily spooked by the rattle of staging, were back again. Two of them. A pair, Ernie hoped. "Could I borrow your dog?" he asked Mr. Little, whose eyebrows shot up in a question. "Just for a minute," Ernie explained. "For the picture. We get my wife's dog over here and bingo, I got animals two by two. Two birds, two dogs. What else would God need?"

Mr. Little whistled at the city car and out jumped Junie, thundering through the open window, her back end waggling back and forth with her tail. Marie was up now, too, hobbling down the porch stairs, Pumpkin Pie trotting ahead of her, beelining toward Junie's yellow tail. As the dogs sniffed each other, Ernie loped across the grass to help Marie navigate the bumpy spots. "Didn't come to me before now," he told her, "but these dogs are just the ticket." He gentled her over the uneven grass and introduced her to Mr. Little. "This fellow's donated his dog to the occasion."

Marie held hard to Ernie's arm. She offered her free hand to the pink-tongued Junie and cooed at her. Mr. Little seemed pleased, and didn't hesitate a second when

Ernie asked him to lead the dogs up the plank and order them to sit. They did. Then Ernie gathered Marie into his arms—she weighed nothing, his big-boned girl all gone to feathers—and struggled up the plank, next to the dogs. He set Marie on her feet and snugged his arm around her. "Wait till the birds light," he cautioned. Mr. Little waited, then lifted the camera. Everybody smiled.

IN THE wintry months that followed, Ernie consoled himself with the thought that his ark did not win because he had misunderstood the guidelines, or that he had neglected to name his ark, or that he had no experience putting into words that which could not be put into words. He liked to imagine the panel of judges frowning in confusion over his written material and then halting in awe at the snapshot—holding it up, their faces all riveted at once. He liked especially to imagine the youngsters in the art office, the redheaded girl and the boy with rings, their lives just beginning. Perhaps they felt a brief shudder, a silvery glimpse of the rest of their lives as they removed the snapshot from the envelope. Perhaps they took enough time to see it all—birds lighting on a gunwale, dogs posed on a plank, and a man and woman standing in front of a little door, she in her bathrobe and he in his greens, waiting for rain.

At the Mercy

HENRY JOHN MCCOY, *CEO,*
Atlantic Pulp & Paper

I am not a patient man. My daughter is reading poetry, aloud, in the seat next to me, because (she says) she has always loved poetry. Her mouth opens and closes over the words—wide, narrow, wide, narrow—which is either the way people read poetry aloud these days or a signal to me that she suspects I might be unfamiliar with words like *urticant* or *sidereal*, which I am. My daughter's abiding love of poetry is one of many facts that I have not (she says) managed to apprehend about her character, either because I was never home (which is true) or didn't give a sweet goddamn about the machinations of her inchoate soul. She says.

Why I agreed to this trip in the first place, I cannot say. I've got a paper mill famously on strike; a fleet of overpaid lawyers getting their intestines rearranged by a couple of crew-cut federal-type mediators in cheesy suits; a cabal of accountants secretly floating trial balloons to South African buyers; and a squadron of attorneys sifting every United States labor case since 1870 through an extremely fine sieve so that if I'm forced to fire the seven hundred replacement workers I hired eight months ago I can find a way to cut the damn place loose and stay out of jail in the meanwhile.

In a word, I've got problems.

Am I back at my office, badgering my spokesmen to come up with a sound bite the press can't convert to nitroglycerin? No. What I am doing is looking for an exit off 95-North, in search of the country inn among the pines where my daughter claims we shall divest ourselves. Of what, I have no idea. Our shoes, is what I hope. Our cell phones. But I have known my daughter a long time, twenty-six years, long enough to understand that what she is on is a mission, and that her mission is not simple. Or, rather, that she is on a mission simple to her but impenetrable to me.

This so-called poetry is the musing of a Vietnamese lesbian activist whose name contains diphthongs that ought to carry dental insurance. "I don't get it," I tell my daughter, suddenly bent on infuriating her, which, I confess, is part of my character, to infuriate people just to see what they will do. My daughter calls this habit of mine a demonstration of unresolved hostility toward my repressed Irish Catholic parents, God rest their repressed Irish Catholic souls. I have come a long way using this technique, and only recently has it turned out to bite me on the backside. My daughter looks up, studies me for a wordless moment as if I were a road sign she finds interesting but irrelevant, and goes on reading without a discernible pause in the narration.

After two more stanzas, if that's what you can call them, she lowers the book and sighs. "What don't you get, Daddy?" Part of her mission, apparently, is to call me Daddy for the duration, which she has not done, to my recollection, since second grade. This is a diversionary tactic that is working splendidly. She used to call me Henry, like everybody else. This "Daddy" business has me flummoxed, I'll admit.

"Her metaphors are so gloomy," I suggest, "what with all the blood and barbed wire and urticants and so on. Maybe she'd have a better time of it in her own language."

My daughter slams down the book. "She happens to be an *American*, Daddy, just like you."

"I hardly think she's just like me, sweetheart."

"You made this assumption, is what I'm saying."

I adjust my seat a little, just to try out the bells and whistles on this, the shark-colored Mercedes I paid way too much for; no doubt the repressed Irish Catholic parents against whom my daughter claims I am demonstrating unresolved hostility did a pirouette in their two-for-one grave.

"I like poems that rhyme," I say, sounding more old-mannish than I expect to. Because I am forty-nine years old and the CEO of an outfit that owns five paper mills, my daughter believes my sensitivities have been blunted, that I wouldn't know a sonnet from a status report. Before she can get on her high prancing horse, I add, "Such as Dickinson. Longfellow. Frost. Shakespeare. Rhymers all." Then I quote all four stanzas of "The Road Not Taken" to press the point.

"You wouldn't be so damned amused if you'd had your country defoliated by a bunch of criminals."

"I thought you said she was American."

"I'm talking about her ancestors. It's the same thing. Sorrow has a way of seeping down through generations."

"Don't blame me, I protested that war."

"By hanging a banner from your dorm room on Harvard Square?"

This little exchange is only one demonstration of the dangerous nature of this trip. In fact, my daughter is furious with me for a labor strike over which I have lost control. For eight endless months—the exact duration of the final rotation in my daughter's Ph.D. program in psychology—I have been engaged in a cockfight with a rock-solid labor union in Abbott Falls, Maine. Clearly my daughter has spent too much time watching the news and not enough time on her studies, because this excursion strikes me as therapeutically suspect, the sort of thing that could attract a juicy malpractice suit were she to try this with a real patient. And the fact that she's been reading aloud Asian poetry instead of Woody Guthrie lyrics makes me very, very nervous. I have a sixth sense for a trap, and it's kicking in right now as she jams the poetry book into the side pocket of my luxury-leather interior.

And then I'm thinking of that lesbian Vietnamese-American poet and the notion my daughter has that one's ancestors' woes translate through the generations. I have a moment of sympathy for both of them, but especially for this daughter of mine whose only apparent goal is to reveal to me the chalk-white soil of my arid inner life. She is a grown woman who from all accounts can orchestrate with skill and conviction and extraordinary kindness the therapy of bulimics and borderlines and bipolars and maybe even a few bunged-up-in-the-ordinary-way stragglers, but when faced with her own father becomes fixed and judging and short of compassion. I know she feels this now, because I, as a child of parents myself, experienced it once. Only parents can reduce you like this. Maybe it's even their job.

"Everybody writes about despair," I tell her. "How about a nice little poem about candles?"

"Pull over," she says, "I'm hungry." Hoping she might give me a reprieve for obedience and cut the weekend from two nights to one, I pull docilely into the parking lot of her choice and escort her into a shabby diner with air you could spread on toast.

The waitress is a hollow-eyed coatrack with hair that looks burned at the ends. My daughter is pleased at this turn of events, pleased with the poor woman's long-suffering shuffle and the way she slips two menus onto our table in a low, underhand slide that no doubt mimics the way she slips her fingers under the Plexiglas divider that separates her from her penitentiary-dwelling husband during their weekly visit; I imagine she's encoded this gesture so far into her muscle memory that she knows no other way to move her hands.

Yes, sir, my daughter is pleased, because I do not frequent places like this as a rule, and she claims I have lost touch with what she refers to as the common man. What my daughter knows about the common man could fit into the little black zipper compartment of her Prada bag. Her mother and I raised her in Montauk, where she took voice lessons and drove her own boat and subsequently trotted off to, respectively, Harvard (B.A., History), Columbia (M.S., Psychology), and Tufts. My daughter is a smart woman—she entered college at sixteen—but not in any useful way that I can see. In this sense I failed her more severely than my own parents failed me.

What my daughter believes about the common man is that the common man wants nothing more than respect and recognition. Plus a roomy dining-room table on which to feed his five noble, sad-eyed children whose superior intelligence shall never be known because of people like me intent on keeping the tired tired, the poor poor, and the masses huddled. Unlike me, however, my daughter has never been a common man. What the common man wants is money, and that's all she wrote.

"I hate you, Daddy," my daughter says to me after we order grilled cheese and coffee. "I hate you so much right now."

"Well, there's something. There's a word I understand."

"I love you, too." Her eyes begin to water and I'm hoping she won't choose this moment to make a scene. She was an even-tempered girl until she fell in with all these mentors and program evaluators. "It's very hard to talk to you, Daddy. You don't understand how closed off you are, how totally withholding."

"Well, I'm sorry," I tell her. Which I'm not. What I am is tired and worried and thinking of a meeting in New York where some asshole mediators are putting my balls in a vise and I'm not even there to say Ow. I am trying to be a good father.

"How's Garrett?" I ask pleasantly, referring to her fish-fingered also-ran of a fiancé.

"Fine," she says. "You don't address me by name, Daddy, have you ever noticed that?"

I have noticed that. I am in fact deliberate about that, and if she were such a crackerjack first-in-her-class future therapist it may have occurred to her that she has the same name as her mother, and that when I address her by her mother's name I feel as if I'm embroiled in one of Emily's old battles, with rules and exceptions and loopholes that make running five paper mills feel about as daunting as calling the numbers at a church bingo. It might also have occurred to her that because I had come to despise her mother at the time she died, I keep forgetting that what my daughter still feels is a wallop of grief, which is simpler, I'm guessing, than the messy assault of thoughts that visited me when I heard of Emily's sudden death.

I didn't say I was a wonderful man, only that I was trying to be a good father.

"Is this it?" I ask.

"Is this what?" my daughter asks.

"Is this what you brought me along for, to eat in a punky diner and tell me you hate me?"

She narrows her eyes, which reminds me, as I have been reminded eerily often since we got into the car in front of my office on West Fifty-Seventh Street early this morning, of my dead ex-wife. When I saw my daughter flagging me at the corner, I thought with all my heart that she was my wife Emily of long ago, that lovely, tender-lipped brunette who had a way of reeling toward you as if compelled by unknowable forces to reach a destination just beyond your own shoulders. My daughter Emily, like my wife Emily before her, has not once put enough clothing on her body. Against this cold October day— forty-five degrees at eight this morning—this day on which we were to head north, she armored herself with a flimsy sweater and a pair of sandals. Seeing my daughter do this, the heels of her sandals clicking madly on the sidewalk, I recalled reluctantly that I once loved the original Emily so much that the first time she refused to marry me I stayed up all night weeping beside the dirty river that divided the pitiful towns we came from.

"I said I loved you, too," my daughter tells me.

"So noted."

The waitress, whom I now suspect of suffering from the final stages of cancer or TB, brings us each a flat, oozing grilled-cheese sandwich with a side of chips that she delivers with that same underhand slide.

"What's your name?" my daughter asks her.

The waitress's eyebrows, two wavy penciled lines, lift. "Randi," she says. "With an *i*."

"Randi, this lunch looks delicious," my daughter says. "Thank you, Randi."

The waitress swallows what I take to be a bellow of repressed laughter and whisks away. Suddenly I feel like one of my daughter's experiments, and I remember, for no reason I can unravel, since I have talked to my daughter only twice since the commencement of a labor action that has me eating Tums like peanuts all day long and half the night, that her dissertation is something about modeling. As in "being an example." As in taking socially backward, therapeutically challenged individuals who are stuck halfway between an institution and a garden party, and bringing them into the world by baby steps with the intention of "modeling" decent, socially correct behavior without adding the stress of direct instruction.

"That was Mom's dissertation," my daughter snaps at me when I point out my discovery. Then she narrows her eyes again. "My dissertation is about something else entirely."

For the next fifteen minutes, which pass in prickly silence, I feel—well, I don't know how I feel. The words that come to mind are my daughter's words, and Emily's words before her, squishy therapy words like *vulnerable* and *exposed*. I feel the way I used to feel going shopping for shoes with my mother, afraid of meeting anyone I knew, afraid of their knowing how my mother shopped: get the cheapest pair one size ahead, after which I would spend three-quarters of the school year goose-stepping to keep the shoes on.

"All right, then. What *is* your dissertation about?" I ask, believing I know the answer already. Her dissertation is about me. About my failure as a father. About my meeting in Tokyo that, unfortunately, coincided with her mother's funeral. I appear in disguise, of course, as a modality or paradigm shift or some other grad-school ga-blah. For a moment I fear she might have brought it with her, that the purpose of the trip is to corner me into reading an analysis of my fatherly absence, how it turned her into a person who can't make anything easy, not a simple phone call, not an announcement of marriage, not the caretaking arrangements at her mother's grave site, not the ordering of a truly hideous grilled cheese.

"I'm not at liberty to discuss my dissertation," my daughter says loftily. "It's groundbreaking stuff. I've been advised to keep it secret."

I don't like secrets. I drink the rest of my coffee, which tastes faintly of dish soap, and get up. "You done?"

She gets up. We have both eaten everything on our plate, like two kids on a first date displacing their other appetites. It strikes me that my daughter and I must be experiencing something like that kind of ferocity, an intent to devour each another in ways we have yet to fathom. I leave a twenty on the table, ostentatiously, an aggressive show of generosity. I learned a long time ago that the best defeat is to give the enemy exactly what he has asked for in a way that makes him sorry to have wanted it. "A twenty?" she says. "That's a twelve-dollar tip."

I saunter to the register and pay the bill again, then tell her, "Actually, it's a twenty-dollar tip."

Outside she stops me. "That was insulting, Daddy. The woman's not a charity case."

"I was being nice," I tell her.

"No you weren't," my daughter says. "You were making a show." She follows me to the car, steaming. "It's about interrogating our assumptions," she adds. "My dissertation. That's all I can say."

Words like this usually go in one ear and float into the

oblivion of my subconscious, emerging at odd moments, for instance at a cocktail party or an annual meeting. In this case I do not wish to understand what assumptions my daughter is interrogating. Not now, not at a party six months hence.

She stops in front of my new car with her arms folded, assessing the license plate, which reads PAPRMKR.

"You don't make paper, Daddy," she says coolly. "They do. Or did." Then she gets in on the driver's side. "May I drive?" Of course she is testing me.

"Sure," I say, tossing the keys in after her. We're a half hour away; how much damage can she arrange in half an hour? I remain for a moment in the bracing wintry breath of this autumn day, wishing I'd become a weatherman back when I still had choices. To watch the sky and know what it means would be a magical talent indeed.

I open the passenger door. "'I shall be telling this with a sigh,'" I say, summoning once again the Frost poem I've committed to memory.

My daughter stares ahead. "I heard you the first time."

I settle into the passenger side, and here's a surprise: it's comfortable. I adjust the seat, working the controls until I feel strangely off my feet. Just as I remember the salesman's description of this seat's having a "cradle setting," my daughter begins to sing.

This I had forgotten. This I had completely forgotten, that my daughter has the voice of a fallen angel, vocal cords made of silk and smoke. And I think again of my daughter's notion of ancestry, of handed-down sorrow. Could she believe I exist someplace in those shadowy notes, that whatever operates the heart-lifting thrum of her throat might hail in part from some veiled, sorrowful part of me? She is singing something from church, I believe, a Negro spiritual, not one of the well-known ones, the type of music designed to make committed pagans fall to their knees. An old feeling falls over me, something I had nearly forgotten, and that feeling is surrender. I do not mean the type of surrender that marked my confusing jig-and-reel through childhood to the drum-beat of my parents' square-shouldered righteousness. That was a surrender of the sort I could overpower, given enough time in the world. No, this is another feeling altogether, reminiscent of seeing a newborn girl, a fearsome melting as you hold her harmless, quivering weight. A terrible dwindling, a long, terrible glance back at who you were just ten minutes ago, before this small, smeared, squalling mass of girl slipped into the waiting world. Her first note, that vocal emanation of outrage, had traces of the vibrato I hear now. The devastating sweetness of it, like warm milk poured from a pan, overtakes me, and the day seems to haze over as a low, protecting cloud. As the fall-blazing trees begin to thicken at the roadsides and the car smoothes us over roads that begin to curve and wind, her words dim, the notes run together, and I am hers, I am helpless before her, and the car fills with an ambiguous, beautiful noise that despite my desire to be led elsewhere, anywhere, leads me harmlessly into sleep.

WHEN I wake, I ask her where we are, surprised by the feeling of being in her hands—of being in any woman's hands, of being at the mercy. My silver-throated captor closes her lips and keeps driving. The weather has shifted mightily, the temperature up fifteen degrees, a low, dense sky with unnerving shrouds of fog moving in and out of our sight. Through the haze I recognize the shirred ridges of evergreens, the crimson-and-gold hills that slope into a valley, the smokestacks chuffing at the valley's heart. We're in Abbott Falls, Maine, yes sir, home of Atlantic Pulp & Paper's northernmost mill. I've been here twice in eight months, and have yet to experience an unguarded moment within its leafy borders. It looks a lot like the town I grew up in, which I suppose my daughter knows. We cruise up and down the glum streets, past listing roofs and hopeful squares of lawn on which rain-spotted FOR SALE signs stand like hostesses at a bad restaurant. "This was your plan all along?" I ask her.

"No," she says, easing my car down one humble street after another. "The plan was to hole up in a B&B, admire some foliage, and figure out how we got to the point where you couldn't be bothered to fly back for my mother's funeral."

"You told me it was all right, Emily," I say, and her name clangs in this troubled northern air. Emily. It sounds foreign and untried. "Emily, you gave me permission."

"And you took it," she says. "That's how little you ever knew me."

Except when you sang, I want to say. Or, I *want* to want to say. I felt like a child when you sang, and also grateful that you were my child. I did.

Instead I say, "I don't see what you hope to accomplish here."

"Well, I see that now," she snaps. "I know how stupid I was to think we could fix everything in a weekend."

"So this is Plan B? Cruise enemy territory in a brand-new Mercedes?"

She shakes her head. "I couldn't bear to stop, so I just kept driving." She pulls over about a block from the mill gate, where I can see an idle picket line. I glance at the glowing face of my watch. It's mid-shift, thank God, so the line is quiet, a small pack of people, all men, holding signs loosely across their shoulders, the smoke from their cigarettes rising around the veiny, burned-looking skin of their faces.

These people are not, as my daughter believes, noble and bereaved, forced by circumstance to occasionally do the wrong thing. That is a description I find myself wishing she could reserve for me. What these men are is desperate, enraged, and a hair's breadth from violence. They are also shrewd, they read the papers, they follow their own fates with the practiced eye of a stockholder. They know the players, the rules, and how those rules have been pretzeled into legal documents that they naturally perceive as having been tipped exclusively in my favor.

"They're tired," my daughter tells me. "They're hard-bitten and lost. What they want is so ordinary. Don't you see that, Daddy?"

"The one on the end. Blue-and-red jacket."

"What about him?" She's suspicious now.

"He bought your braces."

She sits back in the driver's seat and folds her arms, staring ahead.

"The one right next to him paid for your voice lessons. His son footed the bill for Harvard."

"Don't make me your accomplice, Daddy."

"If you want to interrogate some assumptions, my girl, you can start with your own innocence. Why don't you boycott paper until this is over, put off your dissertation for a few months?"

"You have an answer for everything, don't you?"

This is not true. I do not have an answer for my daughter, Emily. I have never had an answer for her, except that I fear her, or rather the ache that comes from recalling the one way I really did fail her: I folded her in with the other Emily and abandoned them both. She did not have to spirit me to the scene of my alleged crimes to teach me this.

All at once the gate lights come on, activated by the darkening mist. The picket line stirs lightly, a hint of motion that appears to me rife with menace. It is then I remember my vanity plate, the one my daughter sneered at, the one that has been made much of in the news. A sound comes from their midst, a shout of uncertainty mixed with outrage, then the sound takes the shape of a question and the small, edgy pack shifts toward us with the precision of birds changing direction and my daughter is making a sound like a surprised squirrel.

"Start the car, Emily," I say. I try messing with the buttons to get out of the cradle of this seat and can't find the right ones, end up in a perfect position to be stabbed in the belly if someone so desired. "Emily. Start the car."

They are upon us now, a ring of faces peering at us

from the murk, about six of them, backlighted by the safety lights around the gate, their faces feverish and easy to interpret. I start jabbing buttons at random, trying to get myself worked into a more manly pose. My window sinks soundlessly down.

I hear my name, hear some expletives and two or three obscenities entirely new to me and regional in a way I didn't expect. I admit my identity. I tell them just who I am. Out of nowhere, like a magician's trick, they produce a couple of baseball bats, fine blond small bats of the sort you might see on a Little League field.

"Oh my God Daddy oh my God Daddy," my daughter is calling, and then the sound of the revving motor fuses with the first downward chop of a bat on the hood and my daughter's high-pitched squeal. The fog lifts and lowers, lifts and lowers, and I see them in pieces—a frayed shirttail, a tuft of hair, a twisted lip. I see a raised arm, the rounded tip of a bat, then hear the splintering of one six-hundred-dollar headlight. For a few moments there is nothing but sound, an enraged battering, high cries inside the car and low grunts and murmurs outside, the nails-on-chalkboard grind of the engine, which my daughter is trying to turn over and over, not realizing it's already on. She is banging on the console, engaging the wipers, the locks, the air-conditioning, as the windows rise and fall. Finally there is silence. The men stop. My shrieking daughter turns the wheel and the men stand back with no more passion than if we were a taxi pulling away from the curb.

They broke only one headlight. They creased the hood

in such a way that the engine was not damaged. They pleated the sides and roof and trunk, but not enough to spring the doors. They left the tires alone. They gave me plenty to get home on, plenty else to think about. They damaged me in such a way that I would not be apt to tell. I believe they mistook my daughter for a girlfriend, a prize package I picked up at an awards dinner or theater opening; their intention was to compromise my manhood, not my fatherhood. It is then that I see what I have on my hands, that my predicament will last longer than I thought, that I am up against not the nobility that my daughter will insist on recalling after her hands stop quaking and we are well on our long way home, but rather the bone-deep stubbornness of men with only one path up against a man who appears to have many.

"I thought they might kill you," my daughter says as we cross the border back into New Hampshire and feel safe enough to search for a motel. We are tired, it is dark, I have long since taken the wheel.

"No," I assure her. "They were making a point."

"I'm sorry, Daddy. I had no idea." She wipes her eyes but they keep gushing; she has always cried this way, like her mother, in rivers. "I thought they were going to kill you, Daddy. Really. I thought they would pull you out of the car and kill you and I wouldn't be able to do anything to stop them."

I pull into the parking lot of a decent-looking motel, the kind with an attached restaurant that specializes in fried fish and kiddie plates. "Garrett and I broke up," she says, reaching over me to turn off the ignition. A chuffing sound beneath the hood can portend nothing but trouble. "And I dropped out of my program. No doctorate for me, Daddy." She looks at me, her eyes shiny in the neon reflection of the motel sign, expecting something that I am uniquely unable to deliver. I find myself hoping, God help me, to deliver accidentally. "I can't get over Mom, is the thing," she continues. She looks up, eyes brimming. "Garrett got tired of this."

My daughter waits as I grope for something to say. "He should have helped you," I manage.

She unbuckles herself and picks up her purse. "He didn't cherish me. No man has ever cherished me."

"Well, he should have. He certainly should have."

"He didn't. So I'm telling you. There's a hole in my life that I'm falling straight through. I'm in trouble, Henry, and you're all I've got."

My name sounds flat and sad. She grimaces in such a way—a twist of her soft mouth, smooth, elegiac—that I lose a little breath.

"You're it, Henry," she says. "It was either call you or check myself into a hospital. I'm really sorry." Just when I think I'm close to understanding what she's apologizing for, she adds, "You should've produced that sister I wanted. Then you'd be off the hook and she'd be on."

I look into her shiny, wide-set eyes. Another Emily. Imagine.

"I've been seeing a shrink," Emily admits. "This trip was all his idea." She laughs this awful, humorless laugh. "Obviously he doesn't know us."

I fumble out of the car and open her side. "Come on," I

tell her. "I'll buy you something nice for dinner." She gets out, looking small and baffled in the thickening dark. "This will look a hell of a lot better on a full stomach, Emily, I can promise you that. That I can promise you." I wait for her, considering how I might frame an apology, some careful ordering of words that might cover what I've done without including who I am. What I have in mind requires a fragility of construction that will not appear to me in this hastening moment. Instead, I shepherd her into the motel lobby, thinking to keep my hand on her shoulder, the way I imagine a father would.

That One Autumn

MARIE WHITTEN, *part-time librarian*

She figured to die in summer, then in fall, and now it is winter, a mild one, and she sees that her time has finally come. Everything takes on a pleasant fuzz, like the skin on a peach. For days now she has lain still, staring calmly at her own hands, blue and needle-scarred, folded over her favorite quilt, where her tiny dog slumbers within reach of her fingers. Ernie stays by the window, endlessly glancing back at her, believing she can't die as long as he is watching. In these final hours she has discovered the ability to read his thoughts, and though she is sobered by the expanse of his panic, the bottomless howl he cannot express, she is touched by it, too.

Despite the ice-white sky outside the window, it is not winters past that Marie dwells on, their muffled sense of safety, the cold stars, the hall closet straining with the wet-wool scent and weight of the tangled coats of her husband and son. Instead, it is autumn she thinks of, one autumn in particular, when for a time the days felt like these days: upside down, fraught with meaning.

That one autumn, Marie headed up to the cabin alone. From the first, something looked wrong. She took in the familiar view: the clapboard bungalow she and Ernie had inherited from his father, the bushes and trees that had grown up over the years, the dock pulled in for the season. She sat in the idling car, reminded of those "find the mistake" puzzles James used to pore over as a child, intent on locating mittens on the water-skier, milk bottles in the parlor. Bent in a corner somewhere over the softening page, her blue-eyed boy would search for hours, convinced that after every wrong thing had been identified, more wrong things remained.

Sunlight pooled in the dooryard. The day gleamed. The gravel turnaround seemed vaguely disarranged. Scanning the line of spruce that shielded the steep slope to the lake's edge, Marie looked for movement. Behind the thick mesh screen of the front porch she could make out the wicker tops of the chairs. She turned off the ignition, trying to remember whether she'd taken time to straighten up the porch when she was last here, in August, the weekend of Ernie's birthday. He and James had had one of their fights, and it was possible that in the ensuing clamor and silence she had forgotten to straighten up the porch. It was possible.

She got out of the car and checked around. Everything looked different after just a few weeks: the lake blacker through the part in the trees, the brown-eyed Susans gone weedy, the chairs on the porch definitely, definitely moved. Ernie had pushed a chair in frustration, she remembered. And James had responded in kind, up-ending the green one on his way out the door and down to the lake. They'd begun that weekend, like so many others, with such good intentions, only to discover anew how mismatched they were, parents to son. So, she had straightened the chairs—she had definitely straightened them—while outside Ernie's angry footsteps crackled over the gravel and, farther away, James's body hit the water in a furious smack.

She minced up the steps and pushed open the screen door, which was unlocked. "Hello?" she called out fearfully. The inside door was slightly ajar. *Take the dog*, Ernie had told her, *it'll be good company*. She wished now she had, though the dog, her first Yorkie, was a meek little thing and no good in a crisis. *I don't want company, Ernie. It's a week, it's forty miles, I'm not leaving you*. Marie was sentimental, richly so, which was why her wish to be alone after seeing James off to college had astonished them both. *But you're still weak*, Ernie argued. *Look how pale you are*. She packed a box of watercolors and a how-to book into her trunk as Ernie stood by, bewildered. *I haven't been alone in years*, she told him. *I want to find out what it feels like*. James had missed Vietnam by six merciful months, then he'd chosen Berkeley, as far from his parents as he could get, and now Marie wanted to be alone.

Ernie gripped her around the waist and she took a big breath of him: man, dog, house, yard, mill. She had known him most of her life, and from time to time, when she could bear to think about it, she wondered whether their uncommon closeness was what had made their son a stranger.

You be careful, he called after her as she drove off. The words came back to her now as she peered through the partly open door at a wedge of kitchen she barely recognized. She saw jam jars open on the counter, balled-up dish towels, a box of oatmeal upended and spilling a bit of oatmeal dust, a snaggled hairbrush, a red lipstick ground to a nub. Through the adjacent window she caught part of a rumpled sleeping bag in front of the fireplace, plus an empty glass and a couple of books.

Marie felt a little breathless, but not afraid, recognizing the disorder as strictly female. She barreled in, searching the small rooms like an angry, old-fashioned mother with a hickory switch. She found the toilet filled with urine, the back hall cluttered with camping gear, and the two bedrooms largely untouched except for a grease-stained knapsack thrown across Marie and Ernie's bed. By the time she got back out to the porch to scan the premises again, Marie had the knapsack in hand and sent it skidding over the gravel. The effort doubled her over, for Ernie was right: her body had not recovered from the thing it had suffered. As she held her stomach, the throbbing served only to stoke her fury.

Then she heard it: the sound of a person struggling up the steep, rocky path from the lake. Swishing grass. A scatter of pebbles. The subtle pulse of forward motion.

It was a girl. She came out of the trees into the sunlight, naked except for a towel bundled under one arm. Seeing the car, she stopped, then looked toward the cabin, where Marie uncoiled herself slowly, saying, "Who the hell are you?"

The girl stood there, apparently immune to shame. A delicate ladder of ribs showed through her paper-white skin. Her damp hair was fair and thin, her pubic hair equally thin and light. "Shit," she said. "Busted." Then she cocked her head, her face filled with a defiance Marie had seen so often in her own son that it barely registered.

"Cover yourself, for God's sake," Marie said.

The girl did, in her own good time, arranging the towel over her shoulders and covering her small breasts. Her walk was infuriatingly casual as she moved through the dooryard, picked up the knapsack, and sauntered up the steps, past Marie, and into the cabin.

Marie followed her in. She smelled like the lake.

"Get out before I call the police," Marie said.

"Your phone doesn't work," the girl said peevishly. "And I can't say much for your toilet, either."

Of course nothing worked. They'd turned everything off, buttoned the place up after their last visit, James and Ernie at each other's throats as they hauled the dock up the slope, Ernie too slow on his end, James too fast on his, both of them arguing about whether or not Richard Nixon was a crook and should have resigned in disgrace.

"I said get out. This is my house."

The girl pawed through the knapsack. She hauled out a pair of panties and slipped them on. Then a pair of frayed jeans, and a mildewy shirt that Marie could smell across the room. As she toweled her hair it became lighter, nearly white. She leveled Marie with a look as blank and stolid as a pillar.

"I said get out," Marie snapped, jangling her car keys.

"I heard you."

"Then do it."

The girl dropped the towel on the floor, reached into the knapsack once more, extracted a comb, combed her flimsy, apparitional hair, and returned the comb. Then she pulled out a switchblade. It opened with a crisp, per-functory snap.

"Here's the deal," she said. "I get to be in charge, and you get to shut up."

Marie shot out of the cabin and sprinted into the dooryard, where a bolt of pain brought her up short and windless. The girl was too quick in any case, catching Marie by the wrist before she could reclaim her breath. "Don't try anything," the girl said, her voice low and cold. "I'm unpredictable." She glanced around. "You expecting anybody?"

"No," Marie said, shocked into telling the truth.

"Then it's just us girls," she said, smiling a weird, thin smile that impelled Marie to reach behind her, holding the car for support. The girl presented her water-wrinkled palm and Marie forked over the car keys.

"Did you bring food?"

"In the trunk."

The girl held up the knife. "Stay right there."

Marie watched, terrified, as the girl opened the trunk and tore into a box of groceries, shoving a tomato into her mouth as she reached for some bread. A bloody trail of tomato juice sluiced down her neck.

Studying the girl—her quick, panicky movements—Marie felt her fear begin to settle into a morbid curiosity.

This skinny girl seemed an unlikely killer; her tiny wrists looked breakable, and her stunning whiteness gave her the look of a child ghost. In a matter of seconds, a thin, reluctant vine of maternal compassion twined through Marie and burst into violent bloom.

"When did you eat last?" Marie asked her.

"None of your business," the girl said, cramming her mouth full of bread.

"How old are you?"

The girl finished chewing, then answered: "Nineteen. What's it to you?"

"I have a son about your age."

"Thrilled to know it," the girl said, handing a grocery sack to Marie. She herself hefted the box and followed Marie into the cabin, her bare feet making little animal sounds on the gravel. Once inside, she ripped into a box of Cheerios.

"Do you want milk with that?" Marie asked her.

The girl nodded. All at once her eyes welled up, and she wiped them with the heel of one hand, turning her head hard right, hard left, exposing her small, translucent ears. "This isn't me," she sniffled. She lifted the knife but did not give it over. "It's not even mine."

"Whose is it?" Marie said steadily, pouring milk into a bowl.

"My boyfriend's." The girl said nothing more for a few minutes, until the cereal was gone, another bowl poured, and that, too, devoured. She wandered over to the couch, a convertible covered with anchors that Ernie had bought to please James, who naturally never said a word about it.

"Where is he, your boyfriend?" Marie asked finally.

"Out getting supplies." The girl looked up quickly, a snap of the eyes revealing something Marie thought she understood.

"How long's he been gone?"

The girl waited. "Day and a half."

Marie nodded. "Maybe his car broke down."

"That's what I wondered." The girl flung a spindly arm in the general direction of the kitchen. "I'm sorry about the mess. My boyfriend's hardly even paper-trained."

"Then maybe you should think about getting another boyfriend."

"I told him, no sleeping on the beds. We didn't sleep on your beds."

"Thank you," Marie said.

"It wasn't my idea to break in here."

"I'm sure it wasn't."

"He's kind of hiding out, and I'm kind of with him."

"I see," Marie said, scanning the room for weapons: fire-place poker, dictionary, curtain rod. She couldn't imagine using any of these things on the girl, whose body appeared held together with thread.

"He knocked over a gas station. Two, actually, in Portland."

"That sounds serious."

She smiled a little. "He's a serious guy."

"You could do better, don't you think?" Marie asked. "Pretty girl like you."

The girl's big eyes narrowed. "How old are *you*?"

"Forty."

"You look younger."

"Well, I'm not," Marie said. "My name is Marie, by the way."

"I'm Tracey."

"Tell me, Tracey," Marie said. "Am I your prisoner?"

"Only until he gets back. We'll clear out after that."

"Where are you going?"

"Canada. Which is where he should've gone about six years ago."

"A vet?"

Tracey nodded. "War sucks."

"Well, now, that's extremely profound."

"Don't push your luck, Marie," Tracey said. "It's been a really long week."

They spent the next hours sitting on the porch, Marie thinking furiously in a chair, Tracey on the steps, the knife glinting in her fist. At one point Tracey stepped down into the gravel, dropped her jeans, and squatted over the spent irises, keeping Marie in her sight the whole time. Marie, who had grown up in a different era entirely, found this fiercely embarrassing. A wind came up on the lake; a pair of late loons called across the water. The only comfort Marie could manage was that the boyfriend, whom she did not wish to meet, not at all, clearly had run out for good. Tracey seemed to know this, too, chewing on her lower lip, facing the dooryard as if the hot desire of her stare could make him materialize.

"What's his name?" Marie asked.

"None of your business. We met in a chemistry class." She smirked at Marie's surprise. "Pre-med."

"Are you going back to school?"

Tracey threw back her head and cackled, showing two straight rows of excellent teeth. "Yeah, right. He's out there right now paying our preregistration."

Marie composed herself, took some silent breaths. "It's just that I find it hard to believe—"

"People like you always do," Tracey said. She slid Marie a look. "You're never willing to believe the worst of someone."

Marie closed her eyes, wanting Ernie. She imagined him leaving work about now, coming through the mill gates with his lunch bucket and cap, shoulders bowed at the prospect of the empty house. She longed to be waiting there, to sit on the porch with him over a pitcher of lemonade, comparing days, which hadn't changed much over the years, really, but always held some ordinary pleasures. Today they would have wondered about James, thought about calling him, decided against it.

"You married?" Tracey asked, as if reading her mind.

"Twenty years. We met in seventh grade."

"Then what are you doing up here alone?"

"I don't know," Marie said. But suddenly she did, she knew exactly, looking at this girl who had parents somewhere waiting.

"I know what you're thinking," the girl said.

"You couldn't possibly."

"You're wondering how a nice girl like me ended up like this." When Marie didn't answer, she added, "Why do you keep doing that?"

"What?"

"That." The girl pointed to Marie's hand, which was making absent semicircles over her stomach. "You pregnant?"

"No," Marie said, withdrawing her hand. But she had been, shockingly, for most of the summer; during James's final weeks at home, she had been pregnant. Back then her hand had gone automatically to the womb, that strange, unpredictable vessel, as she and Ernie nuzzled in bed, dazzled by their change in fortune. For nights on end they made their murmured plans, lost in a form of drunkenness, waiting for James to skulk through the back door long past curfew, when they would rise from their nestled sheets to face him—their first child now, not their only—his splendid blue eyes glassy with what she hoped were the normal complications of adolescence, equal parts need and contempt.

They did not tell him about the pregnancy, and by the first of September it was over prematurely, Marie balled into a heap on their bed for three days, barely able to open her swollen eyes. "Maybe it's for the best," Ernie whispered to her, petting her curled back. They could hear James ramming around in the kitchen downstairs, stocking the cupboards with miso and bean curd and other things they'd never heard of, counting off his last days in the house by changing everything in it. As Ernie kissed her sweaty head, Marie rested her hand on the freshly scoured womb that had held their second chance. "It might not have been worth it," Ernie whispered, words that staggered her so thoroughly that she bolted up, mouth agape, asking, "What did you say, Ernie? Did you just say something?" Their raising of James had, after all,, been filled with fine wishes for the boy; it was not their habit to acknowledge disappointment, or regret, or sorrow. As the door downstairs clicked shut on them and James faded into another night with his mysterious friends, Marie turned to her husband, whom she loved, God help her, more than she loved her son. *Take it back*, she wanted to tell him, but he mistook her pleading look entirely. "She might've broken our hearts," he murmured. "I can think of a hundred ways." He was holding her at the time, speaking softly, almost to himself, and his hands on her felt like the meaty intrusion of some stranger who'd just broken into her bedroom. "Ernie, stop there," she told him, and he did.

It was only now, imprisoned on her own property by a skinny girl who belonged back in chemistry class, that Marie understood that she had come here alone to find a way to forgive him. What did he mean, not worth it? Worth what? Was he speaking of James?

Marie looked down over the trees into the lake. She and Ernie had been twenty-two years old when James was born. You think you're in love now, her sister warned, but wait till you meet your baby—implying that married love would look bleached and pale by contrast. But James was a sober, suspicious baby, vaguely intimidating, and their fascination for him became one more thing they had in common. As their child became more and more himself, a cryptogram they couldn't decipher, Ernie and Marie's bungled affections and wayward exertions revealed less of him and more of themselves.

Ernie and Marie, smitten since seventh grade: It was

a story they thought their baby son would grow up to tell their grandchildren. At twenty-two they had thought this. She wanted James to remember his childhood the way she liked to: a soft-focus, greeting-card recollection in which Ernie and Marie strolled hand in hand in a park somewhere with the fruit of their desire frolicking a few feet ahead. But now she doubted her own memory. James must have frolicked on occasion. Certainly he must have frolicked. But at the present moment she could conjure only a lumbering resignation, as if he had already tired of their story before he broke free of the womb. They would have been more ready for him now, she realized. She was in a position now to love Ernie less, if that's what a child required.

The shadow of the spruces arched long across the dooryard. Dusk fell.

Tracey got up. "I'm hungry again. You want anything?"

"No, thanks."

Tracey waited. "You have to come in with me."

Marie stepped through the door first, then watched as Tracey made herself a sandwich. "I don't suppose it's crossed your mind that your boyfriend might not come back," Marie said.

Tracey took a bite. "No, it hasn't."

"If I were on the run, I'd run alone, wouldn't you? Don't you think that makes sense?"

Chewing daintily, Tracey flattened Marie with a luminous, eerily knowing look. "Are you on the run, Marie?"

"What I'm saying is that he'll get a lot farther a lot faster without another person to worry about."

Tracey swallowed hard. "Well, what I'm saying is you

don't know shit about him. Or me, for that matter. So you can just shut up."

"I could give you a ride home."

"Not without your keys, you couldn't." She opened the fridge and gulped some milk from the bottle. "If I wanted to go home, I would've gone home a long time ago."

It had gotten dark in the cabin. Marie flicked on the kitchen light. She and Ernie left the electricity on year-round because it was more trouble not to, and occasionally they came here in winter to snowshoe through the long, wooded alleys. It was on their son's behalf that they had come to such pastimes, on their son's behalf that the cabin had filled over the years with well-thumbed guide-books to butterflies and insects and fish and birds. But James preferred his puzzles by the fire, his long, furtive vigils on the dock, leaving it to his parents to discover the world. They turned up pine cones, strips of birch bark for monogramming, once a speckled feather from a pheas-ant. James inspected these things indifferently, listened to parental homilies on the world's breathtaking design, all the while maintaining the demeanor of a goodhearted homeowner suffering the encyclopedia salesman's pitch.

"Why don't you want to go home?" Marie asked. "Re-ally, I'd like to know." She was remembering the parting scene at the airport, James uncharacteristically warm, al-lowing her to hug him as long as she wanted, thanking her for an all-purpose "everything" that she could fill in as she pleased for years to come. Ernie, his massive arms folded in front of him, stood aside, nodding madly. But as James disappeared behind the gate, Ernie clutched her hand, and she knew what he knew: that their only son, their first and only child, was not coming back. He would finish school, find a job in California, call them twice a year. James had been waiting since the age of eight to try life solo and was not one to turn back on a promise to himself.

"My father's a self-righteous blowhard, if you're dying to know," Tracey said. "And my mother's a doormat."

"Maybe they did the best they could."

"Maybe they didn't."

"Maybe they tried in ways you can't know about."

Tracey looked Marie over. "My mother's forty-two," she said. "She would've crawled under a chair the second she saw the knife."

Marie covered the mustard jar and returned it to the fridge. "It's possible, Tracey, that your parents never found the key to you."

Tracey seemed to like this interpretation of her terrible choices. Her shoulders softened some. "So where's this son of yours, anyway?"

"We just sent him off to Berkeley."

Tracey smirked a little. "Uh-oh."

"What's that supposed to mean?" Marie asked. "What do you mean?"

"Berkeley's a pretty swinging place. You don't send sweet little boys there."

"I never said he was a sweet little boy," Marie said, surprising herself. But it was true: her child had never been a sweet little boy.

"You'll be lucky if he comes back with his brain still working."

"I'll be lucky if he comes back at all."

Tracey frowned. "You're messing with my head, right? Poor, tortured mother? You probably don't even have kids." She folded her arms. "But if you do have a kid, and he's at Berkeley, prepare yourself."

"Look, Tracey," Marie said irritably, "why don't you just take my car? If you're so devoted to this boyfriend of yours, why not go after him?"

"Because I'd have no idea where to look, and you'd run to the nearest police station." Tracey finished the sandwich and rinsed the plate, leading Marie to suspect that someone had at least taught her to clean up after herself. The worst parent in the world can at least do that. James had lovely manners, and she suddenly got a comforting vision of him placing his scraped plate in a cafeteria sink.

"The nearest police station is twenty miles from here," Marie said.

"Well, that's good news, Marie, because look who's back."

Creeping into the driveway, one headlight out, was a low-slung, mud-colored Valiant with a cracked windshield. The driver skulked behind the wheel, blurry as an inkblot. When Tracey raced out to greet him, the driver opened the door and emerged as a jittery shadow. The shadow flung itself toward the cabin as Marie fled for the back door and banged on the lock with her fists.

In moments he was upon her, a wiry man with a powerful odor and viselike hands. He half-carried her back to the kitchen as she fell limp with panic. Then, like a ham actor in a silent movie, he lashed her to a kitchen chair with cords of filthy rawhide.

"You wanna tell me how the fuck we get rid of her?" he snarled at Tracey, whose apparent fright gave full flower to Marie's budding terror. That he was handsome—dark-eyed, square-jawed, with full, shapely lips—made him all the more terrifying.

"What was I supposed to do?" Tracey quavered. "Listen, I kept her here for a whole day with no—"

"Where's your keys?" he roared at Marie.

"Here, they're here," Tracey said, fumbling them out of her pocket. "Let's go, Mike, please, let's just go."

"You got money?" he asked, leaning over Marie, one cool strand of his long hair raking across her bare arm. She could hardly breathe, looking into his alarming, moist eyes.

"My purse," she gasped. "In the car."

He stalked out, his dirty jeans sagging at the seat, into which someone had sewn a facsimile of the American flag. He looked near starving, his upper arms shaped like bedposts, thin and tapering and hard. She heard the car door open and the contents of her purse spilling over the gravel.

"The pre-med was a lie," Tracey said. "I met him at a concert." She darted a look outside, her lip quivering.

"Do something," Marie murmured. "Please."

"You know how much power I have over my own life, Marie?" She lifted her hand and squeezed her thumb and index finger together. "This much."

He was in again, tearing into the fridge, cramming food into his mouth. The food seemed to calm him some. He looked around. He could have been twenty-five or forty-five, a man weighted by bad luck and a mean spirit that encased his true age like barnacles on a boat. "Pick up our stuff," he said to Tracey. "We're out of this dump."

Tracey did as he said, gathering the sleeping bag and stuffing it into a sack. He watched her body damply as she moved; Marie felt an engulfing nausea but could not move herself, not even to cover her mouth at the approaching bile. Her legs were lashed to the chair legs, her arms tied behind her, giving her a deeply discomfiting sensation of being bound to empty space. She felt desperate to close her legs, cross her arms over her breasts, unwilling to die with her most womanly parts exposed. "I'm going to be sick," she gulped, but it was too late, a thin trail of spit and bile lolloping down her shirtfront.

Mike lifted his forearm, dirty with tattoos, and chopped it down across Marie's jaw. She thumped backward to the floor, chair and all, tasting blood, seeing stars, letting out a squawk of despair. Then she fell silent, looking at the upended room, stunned. She heard the flick of a switchblade and felt the heat of his shadow. She tried to snap her eyes shut, to wait for what came next, but they opened again, fixed on his; in the still, shiny irises she searched for a sign of latent goodness, or regret, some long-ago time that defined him. In the sepulchral silence she locked eyes with him, sorrow to sorrow.

He dropped the knife. "Fuck this, you do it," he said to Tracey, then swaggered out. She heard her car revving in the dooryard, the radio blaring on. Now her eyes closed. A small rustle materialized near her left ear; it was Tracey, crouching next to her, holding the opened blade.

"Shh," Tracey said. "He's a coward, and he doesn't like blood, but he's not above beating the hell out of me." She patted Marie's cheek. "So let's just pretend I've killed you."

Marie began to weep, silently, a sheen of moisture beading beneath her eyes. She made a prayer to the Virgin Mary, something she had not done since she was a child. She summoned an image of Ernie sitting on the porch, missing her. Of James scraping that plate in the college cafeteria. With shocking tenderness, Tracey made a small cut near Marie's temple just above the hairline. It hurt very little, but the blood began to course into her hair in warm, oozy tracks.

Tracey lifted the knife, now a rich, dripping red. "You'll be okay," she said. "But head wounds bleed like crazy." The horn from Marie's car sounded in two long, insistent blasts.

"You chose a hell of a life for yourself, Tracey," Marie whispered.

"Yeah," Tracey said, closing her palm lightly over the knife. She got up. "But at least I chose."

"You don't know anything about me."

"Ditto. Take care."

For much of the long evening Marie kept still, blinking into the approaching dark. She had to pee desperately but determined to hold it even if it killed her, which she genuinely thought it might. She was facing the ceiling, still tied, the blood on her face and hair drying uncomfortably. She recalled James's childhood habit of hanging slothlike from banisters or chair-backs, loving the upside-down world. Perhaps his parents were easier to understand this way. She saw now what had so compelled him: the ceiling would make a marvelous floor, a creamy expanse you could navigate however you wished; you could fling yourself from corner to corner, unencumbered except for an occasional light fixture. Even the walls looked inviting: the windows appeared to open from the top down, the tops of doors made odd, amusing steps into the next room, framed pictures floated knee high, their reversed images full of whimsy, hard to decode. In time she got used to the overturned room, even preferred it. It calmed her. She no longer felt sick. She understood that Ernie was on his way here, of course he was, he would be here before the moon rose, missing her, full of apology for disturbing her peace, but he needed her, the house was empty and their son was gone and he needed her as he steered down the dirt road, veering left past the big boulder, entering the dooryard to find a strange, battered car and a terrifying silence.

"Oh, Ernie," she said when he did indeed panic through the door. "Ernie. Sweetheart. Untie me." In he came, just as she knew he would.

And then? They no longer looked back on this season as the autumn when they lost their second child. This season—with its uneven temperatures and propensity for inspiring flight—they recalled instead as that one autumn when those awful people, that terrible pair, broke into the cabin. They exchanged one memory for the other, remembering Ernie's raging, man-sized sobs as he worked at the stiff rawhide, remembering him rocking her under a shaft of moonlight that sliced through the door he'd left open, remembering, half-laughing, that the first thing Marie wanted to do, after being rescued by her prince, was pee. This moment became the turning point—this moment and no other—when two long-married people decided to stay married, to succumb to the shape of the rest of their life, to live with things they would not speak of. They shouldered each other into the coming years because there was no other face each could bear to look at in this moment of turning, no other arms they could bear but each other's, and they made themselves right again, they did, just the two of them.

"Hold me, Ernie," she says now, lifting her arms just as she did then. He does. He holds her.

The Temperature
of Desire

DAN LITTLE, *electrician*

O n the afternoon in question, we had been on strike
for nine months and counting. It was around four-
thirty, snow in the air. I was on my way to get a
burger with my dog, Junie, feeling dull and thickened,
burdened by what my little brother and I had come to.
Under the darkening sky, the mill looked like a ruined
picnic, a sorry brick blanket at the deep center of the valley. Main Street showed signs of wear: a missing letter at
Dave's Diner, and at Showers of Flowers, which is owned
by my cheerful ex-wife, the storefront featured nothing
but a few carnations headed for the top of some lucky
bastard's cut-rate casket. Beyond that was the long green
arch of Porter Bridge, the river running low beneath it. I
was seized by an urge to stop the car, pitch my clothes,
and hurl myself over the guardrail.

Why not? I asked myself. I'm a divorced man with
no kids; my ex-wife is married to an eggheaded cadaver
who welds scrap metal into giant pretzels and calls it art;

my little brother who once adored me hates my guts. The rocks are bare this time of year, I'll be dead before I know I'm drowning, my sister will take care of the dog.

You get this way. You get to thinking God's got a sticker next to your name. But it's strange, the things that hold us to the earth. Just as I was thinking I could really do it, the water churned up what looked like a lost plank, painted red, maybe six inches wide and about a foot long—part of a front step, maybe, or a kid's wagon. And I thought of this guy I'd met, a pipefitter who'd gone a little over the bend. He was building an ark next to his house over on Randall. An ark. As in Noah. The flood. Animals two by two.

Ernie Whitten, his name was. Ernie was a story I'd come upon by accident, a story I thought Timmy might help me figure out. So I turned left instead of right at the bridge, praying that my little brother hadn't already left for good.

We used to be a close family. Barbecues and birthday parties, lots of bad jokes and belly-laughing, everybody's kids marching in and out of all the kitchens. Excepting Timmy's place on West Main, you could pitch a penny from any one of our doorsteps to another. Then Timmy crossed the picket line, and we went all odd and squirrelly. Elaine and her husband, Bing, wouldn't let him near the kids. Our aunt Lucy fed him a couple nights a week but sent him home early. Sonny lit candles at St. Anne's. Roy, the oldest, who busted his hump in the wood room for twenty-five years, don't even ask. And our dad: let's just say he was probably seizing in his coffin.

Timmy crossed about four months into it, after people had gotten fierce and unpredictable. By then the networks had descended with their lights-camera-action, panning across each shift change, where an army of so-called replacement workers streamed in and out with a police escort like they were visiting royalty and not the mercenary soul-crushing scabs from Georgia that they actually were. Local 20, our union, and the UPIU, the national union, had a lawsuit pending, but you wouldn't catch any of us holding our breath. There'd been some long, violent, failed paper strikes back in the eighties that were supposed to teach us once and for all who we were messing with. But we weren't taking clues this time, we were giving them out.

CNN sent this Barbie doll in a khaki jacket who kept referring to us as America's backbone, which actually flattered certain people, like Roy and Bing for example, who stood next to her in these brand-new denim work-shirts. Roy and Bing tend to dress like schoolteachers when they're not working, cotton shirts and chinos, and Roy usually looks kind of hapless, big hands fluttering loose like a couple of schoolbooks. "Fold your arms," Barbie tells him, so he does, and there he is on the videotape we've got, America's backbone, my big brother the union prez, arms folded over his scratchy denim shirt, delivering some overcooked spaghetti of an opinion about solidarity and corporate barracudas and the Founding Fathers. I love Roy, but the man can't string two sentences together. The viewing public must have thought America's back-bone had slipped a disk. Bing didn't say much, just nodded a lot, looking sort of mean and squinty-eyed, which he is not in real life.

The night he crossed, Timmy came over to Elaine and Bing's to confess before the fact. At the time he was living in the apartment on West Main with that dishrag of a cat he had practically on life support. He'd always been like that, sentimental, still wore a shirt my mother gave him in junior high. I'd like to know if he has that shirt now; that, and the rabbit's foot I gave him for his twelfth birthday. The night he came over to see us at Elaine's, he kept taking the rabbit's foot out, rolling it between his palms like a worry stone. We'd just gotten back from a rally and had turned on the late news to find out what the cameras had caught. The florid face of Henry John McCoy, CEO of Atlantic Pulp & Paper, flared onto the screen, his small mouth working as he stood in front of some Manhattan skyscraper after an acrid negotiation session that had lasted exactly nine minutes.

"The guy has a point," Timmy said, standing between us and the TV.

Bing turned down the sound. "What did you say?" he asked Tim, and then we all got up in a confused shuffle, as if we were at a party and it was time to look over the buffet table.

"Nothing," Timmy said. "He's got shareholders to answer to, that's all." His face seemed flushed; he'd skipped the rally for a date with one of the dimpled girlfriends he'd been auditioning for the role of his future wife.

"Shareholders?" I said. In the entire history of our family I don't believe the word *shareholders* had ever come up in conversation, not even during my father's nightly vocabulary drills back when we were kids, long before Timmy was born. Out came the rabbit's foot again, rolling along his palms.

"I can't afford to wait around anymore," he said. "I'm a short-timer." He'd been in the mill two years, since his high school graduation, a pin-drop of time, and here he was talking to us about waiting. "Danny," he said, turning to me, which he always did in times of uncertainty; I could feel the heat of his confusion trained on me. "They're paying me eighteen bucks an hour, Danny," he said. "How do I explain the strike to some stiff flipping burgers at the mall?" Which is not at all the point, not at all.

"Talk to him, Danny," Elaine said just under her breath. Bing said something, too, that I didn't quite catch. It was so quiet you could hear a rumble of news emanating from the muted television.

"Union's like family," I said finally. "You stick by them even if they're wrong."

"Which they're not," Roy added.

"Which they're not," I said.

Tim has this thing he does, he peers at you from beneath a heavy wave of blondish hair that grazes his eyebrows, as if to remind you that you're worth looking up to. If he says something that doesn't square, you hardly notice it because you're thinking about how if you had a son you'd want it to be him.

"It's a business, not a charity," he said, those gray eyes skimming across us: me, Elaine and Bing, Roy and his wife, Eppy. Sonny was at the union hall manning the phones, and his wife, Jill, was working the food bank with their two boys. The rest of the kids were in bed, either upstairs or next door at Roy's.

"This is the kind of crap they teach in high school these days," Roy snapped. "Like good faith doesn't count, or tradition, or bad knees. We're supposed to give back Christmas shutdown, give back Sunday double-time, subcontract all of Maintenance. We're supposed to take the whipping and thank them for not using a gun."

"I've heard the speech, Roy," Timmy murmured. "All I'm saying is that you can't blame a businessman for wanting all he can get from his capital."

I stared into his upturned face. Instead of wondering what was all this business about capital and shareholders, I was looking for his freckles, which had disappeared without my noticing. His freckles were just flat-out gone, and somehow a man's face had turned up on top of them. Then Elaine said, "Daddy didn't raise us to be somebody's capital," and the shimmy in her voice let what she realized filter down to the rest of us, who were not so quick about people: that our little brother planned to cross that very night, that he was going over there in twenty minutes to sign on for the graveyard shift.

Suddenly I was yelling my head off, fists raised, Elaine pulling on my shirt, the kids waking up and wailing out the bedroom windows. Tim's yelling back at me, and I'm thinking, What the fuck happened to your freckles? Really, this is what I was thinking when I hit him, and you can analyze it all you want. He backed away like a stunned bird, a drip of blood at his lip, like I was some kind of something he didn't recognize. But it was him. He was the one in disguise.

I tore after him, not because I wanted to land another punch but because during our scuffle the rabbit's foot had thumped onto the stiff carpet of Bing and Elaine's breezeway. "Here," I said, catching him near his car. He reared back with his fist cocked but saw at once that I had come back to myself. To my relief—to my great relief—he took the rabbit's foot and returned it to his pocket, where I like to think it remains, and that it reminds him of his twelfth birthday and good luck, our huddled warmth at a campsite on Moosehead Lake, a globe of stars swelling over our heads.

"I'm crossing, Danny," he said. "I want the money. I've got plans."

I lifted my arm to indicate the town, the torn-up families, the enflamed tongues on the picket line. "This is war, little brother."

"I know," he said, nodding, nodding, "I know."

"You *think* you do. Listen to me, Timmy. You're breaking my heart, my man." I cupped his chin, careful not to touch his damaged lip. "Think of Dad."

"Danny," he said, "I didn't *know* Dad." Then he slid into his pickup and drove off.

It's true, he didn't know Dad, and that is his terrible loss. My father—our father, I should say—was fifty-two years old when our mother produced Timmy, a wizened troll with slammed-shut eyes. Tim was born twenty years after Elaine, nineteen years after Roy, seventeen years after Sonny, fifteen years after me. Our father was a faithful man and I miss him still, that machinist who loved scales, everything calibrated, quantified. He measured anger in ounces, surprise in feet, and happiness in degrees Celsius.

The happy scale, he called it. Zero to one hundred. Frozen-solid grief to boiling-over joy. "Son, you're looking at a ninety-nine-point-five," he said of himself as we studied Tim in his cradle. I figured he was hedging his bets with that last half degree: maybe the kid would turn out to be useless with his hands. But it was his own ailing heart our father meant. He died four weeks later, and we froze in that house for years. Our mother never thawed—I don't think there was a day when her personal mercury rose above a degree and a half—so it was left to me to pass Dad's lessons on.

I taught my little brother how to read a micrometer and sharpen a drill bit, but also how to navigate a library, flip an omelette, tell a clean joke. I tested him with Dad's old math drills and word puzzles. I explained the workings of the happy scale, hoping my little brother's life would turn out very, very warm. It never occurred to me to include in Tim's instruction the sin of crossing a picket line.

The cameras stayed awhile, setting up behind the gauntlet three times a day as strikers spit on scabs' pickups and brand-new Buicks, hollering things they'd slap their kids for even thinking. I was there, too. I got in their faces and threatened their babies and told them there was a special ring in hell with their names traced in fire. I didn't do this to my little brother, but I let others do it.

That's the part that shocks you, the parts of yourself you get introduced to when push comes to shove.

Timmy wasn't the only one who crossed, not that it matters. Superscabs, we called them, the ones from our own ranks. There was Earlen Lampry, who surprised exactly nobody by crossing since he came from scum and will be scum till his dying day. There were the Blake brothers and Zoo Pritchett and Millard Thibodeau. There were some guys from the west side, and a few girls, shiftless punks looking for beer money, no sense of obligation, no forebears writing union songs and waiting in the snow for a call-up. Thirty-one in all. Tim was the surprise, though, the one nobody could figure.

The other scabs were imports from the South, easy to hate for all kinds of reasons, their Bubba drawls and new trucks and big, stupid belt buckles with *Elvis* and *Jesus* welded into the clasp. And some of them were black, which inspired a fresh set of vocabulary words on the gauntlet, a turn of events that interested the hell out of the Barbie-doll newslady, who stuck that fuzzy microphone in all the likely faces. Then, there's Timmy on the news, telling her we're not a bunch of racists, just papermakers who want to make paper.

This was a mistake. Tim the Superscab defending his hometown. This was a bad, bad mistake, on national TV, and he seemed to know it, his eyes darting beyond camera range like he was taking cues from someone, when I knew—and I was one of the few to be in a position to, I guess—that what he was doing was second-guessing, changing his mind after it was too late.

Which it was. Even if he'd crossed back over that very night, it was too late. Atlantic Pulp & Paper is a big operation, drawing from at least eight towns, but this town took the brunt, and what's more the mill is right in front of our faces, looming up from the riverbank with its uneven row of windows. It makes a good backdrop, the smokestacks pushing out bluish clouds that look kind of beautiful scraping past the top of the hills. Tim's a small guy, and you could see what they were shooting for: this helpless kid caught in the maw of something more powerful than himself, etcetera. It was no secret whose side Barbie was on, though she did her best to hide it, getting guys like Roy and Bing to pose as America's backbone. She dragged one would-be denim-shirt movie star after another in front of the camera, but the message was that unions had gotten big and crooked, that America's backbone had a whole lot of fat on it, that the sainted corporations had no choice but to put down the screws or move the whole shebang to Guatemala where people don't whine about give-backs. They'd get pictures of us pummeling the cab of some guy's waxed sky-blue pickup or racking up the paint with keys and nails. Sweaty-faced, eyes bulging, neck cords standing out like tree roots, we looked like lunatics out there, a mob of dangerous rabble-rousers who hated blacks and Southerners and were bent on bringing down America the Beautiful just to buy a new snowmobile.

Timmy's moment on camera came right after one of these rabble scenes, which I was watching on the news over at Elaine's with my five-year-old niece, Linney.

"There's Uncle Timmy!" she squeaked, squirming out of my arms. She barreled over to the screen to touch his face. Bing got up to turn off the set. "Wait," I said, "let me see this," and man, I saw it, my stomach fisting as I realized how small and nervous he looked. How young.

"He's fucked," said Bing. Linney roared out to the kitchen to tell Elaine that Daddy was saying bad words again. "Shit," Bing said, heaving himself into a chair. He liked Tim the best of all of us. "Shit. What kinda idiot did your mother raise?"

What could I say? There he was, live and in person, apologizing for the town racists. In the meantime Bing and Elaine's other kids were whooping it up on the street with their cousins in a game of touch football. Bing lurched out to the breezeway and hollered at them: "Kids! Get in here!" I could hear a faint whine of protest from somebody, probably Eddie, Roy and Eppy's oldest, and then another roar from Bing: "I said *now*!" The kids came in and lined up, goggle-eyed. "I don't want trouble visiting this house. Anybody asks you about Uncle Timmy, you tell them he's no part of this family. That's what you say, you understand me?"

The kids—nine boys, this family's loaded with boys—looked at their shoes. By this time Elaine's out there, crying a little, holding Linney by the hand. "You understand me?" Bing repeated. Bing's a big, lovable man, and though the kids aren't exactly afraid of him, they answer when he poses a question. The boys mumbled something or other that sounded more or less like yes but not exactly yes. Tim is twenty years old and they kiss the ground he walks on, just like Tim used to with me, like I used to with my father. "Bing," Elaine said, very softly, "let them go," and the kids shot from the breezeway like bottle rockets.

The next morning Timmy wakes up with SUPERSCAB spray-painted across his landlady's hedge and front stairs. Goes out to start up his truck and finds the tires slashed, the doors jimmied, and a hunk of dog shit on the driver's seat. He tells my aunt Lucy, who tells Elaine and Bing, who tell Roy and Eppy, who tell Sonny and Jill, who tell me, and except for my aunt we decide officially that we're not going to do a goddamn thing about it, that it's his neck he stuck out there when he should've known better.

Tempers were running short, and money. This strange, gray calm had fallen over the town like the eye of a hurricane, and we were hoping the mediators could figure something out before we all got tempted to cross. We all thought it; you know we did. And Tim was out there shoving our worst secret down our throats. How could he not have known that?

I bought Timmy his first white shirt, when he was seven years old and making his First Communion. "I'm riding my bike to South America, Danny," he announced, bow-tied and shoe-shined in the parking lot of St. Anne's. The Host hadn't melted on his tongue before he was imagining himself flying away on the midnight-blue Schwinn I'd given him for the occasion. Even back then he was full of plans.

Don't get me wrong. I *wanted* him to get out. Me, I could've done it, too, I could have gotten out, and I didn't, and that's a whole other story. Timmy was getting out and I was glad. We were all glad. He was our boy.

I froze my backside at sixty-one football games over six seasons. I kept him near me through our mother's wake and funeral. I taught him to drive. Then one day I woke up and he'd turned into a kid who could cross a picket line and talk about capital, and it's like he was saying a chimpanzee could make paper, it's not worth what they're paying you, you're lucky to be working at all. This is what you get for loving a child.

Then, in the fall, eight months in, everything changed. A scab died of heart failure while running the gauntlet in his red GMC pickup. The governor put the National Guard on alert. Three other AP mills—one in Alabama, two in Wisconsin—refused their contracts, the same one we'd rejected, and struck. A week after that, somebody— Tree Liston, is my personal guess—shot up a scab's house on the west side, and that, too, made the nationals. And there was a rumor flying around that the CEO himself, Henry John McCoy, slipped into town one night in a silver-gray Mercedes that got a little treatment with a baseball bat. The guys who supposedly did it are known liars, but in any case the feeble wheels of justice suddenly hit overdrive: on a single afternoon in mid-October, court decisions came raining down left right and sideways. Mostly in AP's favor.

On the following Thursday, the weekly rally thrummed with rumor, anticipation, a whiff of theater. The bleachers, which at this point had begun to show mournful blank spots, teemed anew. But I know Roy, I know how he swallows a lot when he's scared, so I steeled myself for the news he had to deliver: we'd lost the suit; the scabs were legal; we'd all been permanently replaced.

The roar that went up sounded like the final buzzer of a packed-full state championship, with a rageful undercoat. We tore over to the gate for the final shift, singing and hollering and picking up anything we could find—bats, branches, nails, and rocks—and I confess that I felt electrified, thudding with a terrible pulsating current of fury, a solidarity the like of which I had not felt in eight months, and it thrilled and scared me as I rounded the corner to the north gate with the bellowing throng.

Then I remembered my brother, feared for him, and the electricity seizing through me sparked and gave out, just like that, as I spotted the National Guard lined up like sentries at a warring border, which this most certainly was. They had tear gas and black boots and helmets and I secretly thanked God for them, I thanked God.

There was, miraculously, no violence that night, unless you want to measure violence in decibels. We sang and chanted, thrust out our chests, led with our bunched chins, then snaked through the streets until about two in the morning, until we began to scatter, reluctantly, piecemeal, spent and wary. We were still singing, some of us, *Solidarity forever, solidarity forever, the union makes us strong*, but our voices had flattened out, and something else, too, giving our ragged notes the superstitious urgency of whistling in a graveyard. Then there was nothing but a muffled, radiating silence, and a hung moon above our heads, and the smokestacks still emitting their quiet gray signals.

Paper was being made. Every man and woman in that unraveling crowd must have thought what I thought: It's over.

Those of us who had held out till then went scrambling for something to tide us through the meanwhile, which is how I ended up as a part-time code-enforcement officer for the city of Abbott Falls. Nights I kept up with the picket; days I spent not inspecting electrical systems, as I'd hoped, but telling tired, edgy people they couldn't build so much as a garden shed unless they paid the fee and allowed for a twenty-foot setback. In a city car I drove streets I'd known all my life, my dog Junie in the back, which wasn't allowed, looking up addresses in order to tell people something they didn't want to hear after too many seasons of nothing but bad news. And it shocked me how much building was going on: decks, dormers, even a garage or two, all with punky boards, water-stained shingles, windows bought on credit. It was almost like a rain dance, people hoping the illusion of prosperity would conjure a miracle and that the three o'clock whistle would call us all back to our stations.

The job, which I was lucky to get, was not without its wonders: on day two I discovered Ernie Whitten. The man didn't appear to know me, though I recognized him as a pipefitter who used to work on my cousin Lenny's crew. From the look of him—deep lines cragging down his face and a dustbunny of a dog that ticked along at his heels—I figured he'd been ten or twelve minutes from retirement before we struck. He was constructing something out of scrap lumber about four inches from his property line.

"It's an ark," he says to me, and it takes me a while to see it. It was tall enough to require staging and shaped to sink like a stone. He's gone a little nuts, I'm thinking—he's been keeping the neighbors up with floodlights and power tools—just nuts enough to weather the strike and the shutdown and the pension rug being pulled out from under his feet. It occurred to me that I might have channeled my own disappointments into something slightly more constructive than popping my little brother on the mouth.

It took a few minutes to explain to Ernie who I was. When it finally came to him that I was from code enforcement, he folded his arms and clammed up. I didn't take offense: I was too busy wondering why in hell an ark was materializing on a striking pipefitter's lawn. And I was thinking, too, of the boat Timmy made when he was four years old, a clumpy rig made of knockoff Lincoln Logs that he carried everywhere. Timmy's boat would float for one wavering second in his blowup pool, then shimmy painfully to the bottom. "Let me fix it for you, my man," I'd tell him, my pants already wet at the cuffs. "No," he insisted, clutching it to his pink chest, "I like it broken," and there was no talking him out of it.

I didn't think Ernie's ark would float any better than Tim's broken boat, but there he was, defending it against my clipboard and pink papers. He stood with his legs apart, like a sailor at the helm. The tiny dog quaked behind one of his ankles.

"Nice little dog," I ventured, trying to look friendly.

"My wife's," he told me. "She's in the hospital."

"I'm sorry to hear that," I said, putting my clipboard behind my back. "I'm sure she'll be on the mend in no time."

"Doesn't look like it," he said. It didn't take a genius to read between the lines: cancer kills half this town sooner or later. I looked up at the ark, at its odd, intimidating presence, and feared I hadn't lived the right kind of life to be able to understand what it was doing there.

I fell into the habit of cruising by there at night just to watch the man work. I'd park across the street with a sandwich and a Coke, Junie sitting in the back, approving. She's a beautiful old dog, a yellow Labrador retriever with flappy chops that make her look like she's smiling. I got her the day of my divorce, a creaky pound dog hours from doom. Every time Ernie got home from the hospital and set to work, Junie sat up and smiled.

The thing started to resemble a picture in a kids' Bible. He had the roof almost on when the city, which was getting stingy and mean in the strike's wide wake, sent me back there with a summons. The ark was illegal on several fronts, and it was my job to fine the guy and get him to pony up.

His wife had come home. At first I was so happy to see this that I hopped out of the car as if I were their visiting grandson instead of the code guy with bad news. Halfway across the lawn I saw that no bad news I had to deliver could be worse than the news already visiting this house.

She'd been bundled into a chaise lounge on the sunporch, her exposed face whittled down to skin on bone, and all of a sudden I was very sorry that it was too late for me ever to have been with a woman as long as Ernie Whitten had been with her. I'm thinking she's waving at me, her tiny, see-through hand wrenching out from the blankets, but of course it's her husband she sees, standing on the roof of their ark. "I'm sorry, Mr. Whitten," I'm calling to him. "It's my job." He just goes on nailing and hammering and checking the porch every couple of minutes to make sure she's still watching.

This was late November, the weirdest on record. One sunny day right after another, temperatures in the sixties. I'm talking day after amazing day. All of a sudden Ernie sees my camera, with which I'm supposed to gather evidence, and asks me to take his picture. He wants the dog in the picture, too, plus my dog, animals two by two, and while I'm getting the dogs to pose, he gathers up his wife and carries her over the gangplank like it's a wedding threshold. I couldn't help but think of my ex-wife, who was at least trying, starting all over with her sculptor and his kids and her perky flower shop. And Tim, too, saving money for his future marriage to a woman he fully expected to meet. And here was a guy with expectation all behind him, building an ark that had no obvious purpose except to please his wife. I gave him the developing Polaroid and left the premises, summons undelivered.

As if my thoughts had conjured him, Timmy turned up on my doorstep that night, and Christ if I didn't think he was six years old again, bringing some mangled squirrel in from the road. Then I got a better look at the squirrel.

"Jesus," I said.

He sat on my stoop and laid the cat over his knees and bawled like a baby, his narrow shoulders heaving, snot and tears gumming down his face.

"Jesus Christ, Tim," I said. "Who did this?"

"You tell me," he said, though his words were so bollixed up with liquor and despair I could hardly make out what he was saying. I went to touch him, maybe knock him on the shoulder or something, some stumbling motion in the general direction of forgiveness, but he batted my hand away. I was thinking of him at twelve, and sixteen, and he was the same kid now at twenty, minus the freckles—too sensitive for his own good. For the second time in a day I was face-up with a sorrow I had no means to understand. My brother's crime was in wanting to get out so badly he'd step on his brothers' necks to do it. It had cost him big, but he was willing to pay. That's how much he didn't want to end up like me. As much as it hurt me to know this, I couldn't think of a blessed thing I wanted that bad, and a weird, vague, crushed part of me wished I did.

"I'm leaving town," he said, getting up. "I said goodbye to Aunt Lucy, and the rest of you can go rot in hell."

"You can't say that," I said. "Don't."

Timmy turned around, holding the cat against his chest as if it were still alive and settled into its favorite spot on his body. "They've got two-inch-wide minds, Danny," he said. "Sonny and Roy and the rest. They turned you into an old man with a dog." I watched him wend down the road toward his apartment, crying over an animal who'd been half-dead for about two years anyway.

I suppose it could have ended there, and would have, except for that Sunday afternoon, two days later, when I got the urge to jump. The sky hung low and, as I said, snow was in the air. As I considered the down-below rocks, it occurred to me that I'd been watching a man and his wife make their complicated good-bye. Maybe my brother and I owed each other something like that.

When I got to his apartment, he was packing the last of his stuff. "Where are you headed?" I asked him.

He was crating up some camping gear and didn't look up.

"Tim?"

Still no answer. His rapid motions sounded like a beating: *slam, bam, bang.*

"What if something happens, Tim? How do we get in touch with you?"

"Aunt Lucy will know." His forearms flexed mightily as he stuffed a jacket into an already full box. "If you've got something to say, you can tell her."

"I didn't kill your cat," I said.

He continued doing what he was doing, furiously cramming gear into too-small spaces. "You might as well have, Danny," he muttered. "It might as well have been you."

I stood there, in his stripped apartment, feeling hot and choked, as if someone had set fire to my internal organs. "Listen, Timmy," I said. "There's something I'd really like you to see."

Finally he looked at me. And maybe because Junie was with me and appeared to be smiling, he consented to come for a ride.

By the time I parked, snow was coming down in a sloppy, grayish onslaught that was half rain. The ark, alone on the lawn, resting on its flat bottom, looked both finished and abandoned. I kept the engine running, and the heater, and the wipers. I left the radio on low in case we had nothing to say. Junie spread herself across the backseat. I cracked open a beer and handed it to my brother. The car felt cozy, in a way.

"It's not a bad-looking boat," Timmy said, grudgingly. "Kind of tall and beamy."

"I'm supposed to make him take it down. Poor guy's right at zero on the happy scale. Two degrees, maybe, if you count the dog." He didn't say anything, so I kept going: "I've been wondering if maybe God halted the weather fronts or what have you just so this guy could finish a going-away present for his wife."

The car swelled with the ticking wipers, the dog's breathing, and the radio's quiet static. "It's not a going-away present," Tim said quietly.

I flicked off the radio. "What, then?" I really wanted to know.

He shook his head, then took a sip of beer. "Look at that thing, Danny. He's begging God not to take his wife, come hell or—well, or high water. It's like a totem or something. I don't know. A prayer."

"A lot of good it'll do," I said. "I've seen her. She's days from dying, Tim. Hours, even."

"Maybe God spared her. Maybe she's in there right

now trying on some new clothes." He drained the beer. "For all we know they're both so happy the mercury's exploded."

What snow there had been disintegrated into a steady rain. The hulking, useless ark, so heavy with a stranger's strange hope, glistened with water. "For all we know," I told my little brother, "she's already died."

Timmy nodded. "That's the difference between you and me."

I let some minutes tick past. "Write to me, Tim, will you?"

He was looking at the ark. "Come on, Danny," he murmured. "What would I say?"

"Say anything. Hell, just buy a postcard and sign your name."

He nodded. A crisp, deliberate nod, the gesture of a grown man. Our father, whose thoughts contained so little ambiguity, had moved his head in exactly this way.

The rain melted down. Junie was snoring, and the beer was gone. Through the smeared windshield I thought I saw the ark move, a nearly imperceptible rocking at the stern as water pooled beneath it.

"Did you see that?"

"See what?" In the waning light my little brother's eyes appeared older, blunted by the hours.

"I half-believe that thing might float," I whispered.

Timmy sat up, very slowly, the vinyl seat groaning around him. And we waited.

Ernie's ark did not rise up and float away that night. I hope it doesn't matter. I hope what matters is that we believed it might. That we waited there together in the dark. I hope my little brother understood why it was not possible for me to apologize, and that he will remember me, as I will remember Ernie, as one man doing the best he could against uncontrollable forces. This is my hope. Meanwhile I'm the one sending postcards, one every seven days, the way Noah sent his dove in search of dry land.

Hush, Little Baby

CARRIE WHITTEN, *singer*

Carrie looked into Devin's eyes, the same zinger eyes as his famous father. "This is my favorite song," she said. "We can't do one song the way I want?" She put down the mic, clattered to the lip of the makeshift stage, and sat down in the grime. "It's a *lullaby*," she insisted. "For a *baby*. Babies don't enjoy 'edge,' generally speaking."

The song in question was "Summertime," which Carrie had first learned two years ago at the California All-State High School Music Festival. The song meant something to her, especially now, marooned in Bryce, Alaska, in January, where the relentless dark and cold seemed to have shriveled every fellow feeling or inclination toward kindness.

"Here's the thing, Carrie," Devin said, climbing down next to her, guitar still strapped on. Its body dug at her ribs as he slid his arm around her. "You wanna sing your way, I get that totally. I can totally get behind that. But this isn't your band. You're the girl singer. We're inventing something totally new here, and singing lullabies to imaginary babies isn't exactly item one on the Toxic Scream agenda, if you get my meaning." He lit a cigarette. The other guys sensed a protracted detente session and ambled off to the bar, where Lester rang open the cash register at the first hint of movement.

"We're doing this song angry, man," Devin told her, exhaling. "We're taking an American icon and turning it on its big black ass." Then he crushed the cigarette out on the floor; he never smoked beyond the first two drags.

Carrie stared at the mashed cigarette on the filthy floor, not wanting to know what Devin meant by her favorite song's big black ass. His arm weighted her shoulders. It was too hot in this place—Lester's, one of six barrooms in a town with a population of nine hundred, max—and Carrie thought she might pass out. She felt sick again, feared what these bouts of nausea might portend. She shook her head, no, she would not do it his way, she would not splatter out those words in an apoplectic falsetto fashioned to make Ms. Harriman, her high school chorus teacher, seize with outrage. "You can *sing*," she'd told Carrie over and again, and she was right: Carrie could sing. Pitch-perfect, with almost no vibrato, a haunting, monochromatic, milky smoothness that people tended to listen to with their mouths partly open.

But that was then, back when she was Carrie Whitten from Walnut Creek, California. That was before Devin strolled into the Bush Street Starbucks at the end of her shift, gig bag hoisted over his shoulder. He ordered a double espresso, and when he smiled that famous smile once removed, she recognized him: the notorious son of a really, really famous actor. With his beautiful teeth and long, rippling hair he struck her as reckless, groundbreaking, all "edge"—his favorite word. His band needed a girl singer.

After that came the road trip north, the one-night crashes on Devin's friends' balding carpets, the freezing campgrounds, the horrible dog Devin picked up at a rest stop in Tacoma. By the time they reached the Kenai Peninsula the music had gotten out of hand—Carrie been trained by a *spinster*, for God's sake, in a high school chorus that sang straight-ahead, in-the-slot, four-part harmonies.

Now she spent four nights a week at Lester's, shrieking into a microphone as if trying to catch her brain on fire, because Devin's "vision" fused early punk and nineties techno with an "homage-slash-fuck you" to the jazz masters, who would throw up in their coffins if they had but one moment to wake from the dead. With the advancing dark and deepening cold, the music had gotten muddier and weirder and—there was no other way Carrie knew to say it—*violent*, and was it some kind of crime against music history-in-the-making to add a lullaby to their cynical, deaf-making, people-hating repertoire?

"You knew what you were getting into, Carrie," Devin was saying to her. "You knew what we were about."

"Input," she said, spitting the word into the floor. "I thought we were about giving somebody besides you a syllable or two of input."

Devin grunted—it was a certain laugh that he used

at certain times—a sound that startled her unreasonably. His vest still smelled of the smoky campsite north of Cache Creek where they'd shared a sleeping bag that felt like a used skin.

"Take ten," Devin said, though they were already on a break, and weren't even really in rehearsal to begin with. They were just killing time. "Somebody's got to take the dog to the vet anyway," Devin added, meaning: Somebody besides me.

Carrie looked around at the other guys—they'd had it with Devin, and with the dog, who was neurotic and snappy, and with the pathetic money Lester was paying them, and it was only a matter of days, she knew this, before they abandoned Devin and his musical vision and headed back south in Ronny's van, an eventuality she could not bear to consider, not for an instant, it would be like being stranded on the moon, and she couldn't call her mother, whose four favorite words were *I*, *told*, *you*, and *so*. She had three dollars left on the phone card she'd bought before leaving Walnut Creek, and she'd been hoarding it, saving it like prisoners save cigarettes, thinking to put it to use during some emergency she didn't want to predict.

"I'll take the dog," Carrie said. "I'd hate to miss my four allotted seconds of daily sunlight."

She held her palm out to Devin. His eyes were exactly, exactly like his father's, an honest-to-God cornflower blue, though she'd only seen his father's eyes on the big screen, scaled to about forty power. She wiggled her fingers. "You think they treat dogs for free up here?"

Devin pulled out a couple of fifties—he seemed to

have an unlimited supply. The other guys were just beginning to figure out that Devin could put them all up in a
four-star hotel with mints on the pillows—not that such a
thing existed here—if he weren't so hell-bent on looking
"authentic."

She looked at the money laid oafishly across her palm.
Her fingers bore alarming white spots, a sickly dapple at
the tips. A result of the cold, she hoped, or six months
of road food. "Hush little *baby*," she informed him, staring at the white spots. "That's what the song says, Devin.
Hush little *baby*, not Hush little turn-up-the-amp-til-
your-eyeballs-explode." She pocketed the money. "I'll
go straight to hell before I let the son of an *actor* cram
so-called *edge* into this, this *vessel*, just because he thinks
he's the hottest lead guitarist in the Western Hemisphere.
Which he isn't."

The guys started to snicker. Lester stood behind the
bar, smirking—apparently he lived in hope of these little
flare-ups, his sole entertainment in this place that was
missing letters in every single sign: UDWEISE and M LLER
and OP N. Why else would he let the house band while
away entire afternoons in pseudo rehearsal, hogging the
electricity and toking up in the bathrooms?

Devin narrowed those movie-color eyes, giving her a
chill. "I don't care for your attitude," he said, snaking his
fingers around her wrist, hard. "You were more fun before
you got the idea you were fronting the band."

*I was more fun before you started using me like a blowup
doll*, she wanted to say, but didn't. She was scared, and
surprised to be scared, but there it was, finally, the in-

formation she had tucked away since Cache Creek and covered with loud, loud singing: He scared her.

The notion had begun to emerge after last night's gig, when he arranged her on the clammy cot of their bedroom in such a way as to resemble, exactly, the centerfold of a magazine with a name so disgusting she couldn't even pronounce it in her head. We're consenting adults, he said, and she couldn't deny it. After he placed her hands on her own body—*here, here*—he merely looked at her. She moved not a muscle, not an eyelash, it seemed, until he left the room and she heard the locustlike hum of his practice amp warming up. She burrowed into the covers, and then blanked her mind, blanked it, and wished for the thousandth time that on one of these frozen nights, walking the two blocks from this crummy apartment to the overheated steam bath of Lester's, she might catch sight of the Northern Lights, and her stay in this place would not be in vain.

Now she looked at him straight on, like an animal bluffing. "I won't scream it," she said quietly. "I won't scream that song." The sound of her own voice, so spongy and soft, frightened her anew.

"We hired you to scream," Devin said. He gave her another fifty and closed her fingers over the money, forcing her fingers down, one by one. "Lighten up, Carrie. You'll live longer."

Carrie went still. She puffed out her shoulders. Bravado had always been her strong suit, and she hung on to it now as if it had handles. She shook him off, her chin cocked, and shrugged on the coat she'd bought out of desperation at a discount warehouse in Anchorage, a glorified air mattress, puke green, that fell to her ankles and covered most of her hands. Her feet would be cold, given the shoes she was wearing—skinny straps and three-inch heels—but she didn't care, she didn't, she'd convulse in Ronny's van for twenty minutes waiting for the engine to warm up as she scraped ice crystals from the inside of the windshield. Devin's Expedition, strictly off-limits, had a great heater.

She stepped into the pinkish light of midday, cowed by the scenery. In two hours it would be dark again. She'd sent postcards to friends back home telling them about the massiveness of the place, the awe-inspiring, outsized splendor of it all, but in truth the landscape paralyzed her, robbed her of all sense of scale, time, perspective. It was like being on another planet where the laws of physics were hung up somewhere in legislation. She walked the two blocks to the apartment in her flimsy shoes, the one pair of shoes in Alaska that didn't feature big fat ugly Frontierland no-fashion corrugated tracks carved into the soles. It was two degrees below zero out there—an unholy temperature that had the locals bragging how warm it was for January. Well, she'd be chopped into pieces and sent home in a box before two freezing fucking Alaskan degrees would stop her from wearing these shoes, which she'd found on sale for seventy-five percent off. She'd walk all over this frozen avalanche for forty days and forty nights if she felt like it.

By the time she reached the door her toes had gone dead, and the phone was ringing, which always wigged out the dog, a screwed-up cross between a Sasquatch and a polar bear, all white and fangy and unpredictable and paws the size of fur hats. He'd bitten Devin once, Milo twice, and had even snapped at good-natured Keith, who threatened to call the cops, not that anybody in Bryce, Alaska, would care if he did. The dog would have to gnaw the legs off a nun before anybody she'd met here would so much as fill out a complaint form.

She raced inside to get the phone as the dog leapt over the couch and knocked the phone from its cradle. He galloped into the kitchen and back three or four times. Carrie grabbed the receiver and cowered behind the drapes (the dog was petrified of the drapes) and put the phone to her ear.

"Carrie?" It was her mother. "Carrie? What's going on up there? It sounds like you're in the middle of an earthquake."

"It's just the dog," she said, wanting to weep for hearing her mother's voice. "He likes to answer the phone."

"Oh," her mother said, laughing a little—a phony, joyless, covering-up-something laugh. "Look," she said after a few moments. "Your grandmother died yesterday. Your father's here right now. I told him I'd fly to Maine with him."

She could hear the dog ramming himself against the kitchen door, which had latched shut behind him. This happened three or four thousand times a week.

"Grandma died?" Carrie said. She didn't know her grandmother well—her grandparents lived Maine and didn't visit much—but she slid down against the wall and sat, eyeing the pulsating door of the kitchen, overcome.

"You might want to call your grandfather, Carrie. I'm giving you the number."

Carrie spotted a pen entombed in a dust bunny; though she had no intention of calling her grandfather (what would she say?) she took the pen and wrote the number on her hand. She had to scratch the length of her arm a few times to get the ink started.

"Look, how are things up there? Are you still playing that hotel?"

"Yeah," Carrie said. "The rooms are great. They give us pool privileges." She had left home to send a message to her embattled, scorekeeping parents, hoping the name of the band she was taking off with would just flat-out slay her mother, and it did, sort of, but her mother had already been flattened by more pressing matters, namely, trying to divorce Carrie's father without looking like a quitter. And besides, her mother thought Devin's father was the greatest actor of his generation, which softened the blow considerably.

"I really don't see the point of all this, Carrie."

"Bands pay their dues up here. I told you. They come back with reputations."

"That's *him* talking, Carrie. He might as well be moving your mouth for you."

"Look, I've gotta take the dog to the vet. I'm late already."

"Children of the rich and famous think they have nothing to lose, Carrie," her mother said. "Just because his father is generous and intelligent...." But of course she was referring not to Devin's father, but to the generous, intelligent characters he played.

"Mom. Don't."

"Look, do you need money?"

"It's a *gig*, Mom. They pay me." Which wasn't strictly true. Devin kept her money.

"This is a little girl's fantasy, Carrie. You should be in college."

"You told me to get over myself. To grow up. So. Here I am." This was the opposite, the exact opposite, of what she wanted to say.

Her mother sighed. "Call your grandfather. Poor man's been out of work for months, and now this."

"I know."

"Don't mention the divorce. We haven't told him."

"Fine. I won't."

"You don't know what suffering is, Carrie."

"I *said* I'd call."

Carrie hung up, benumbed. She opened the kitchen door and whisked herself inside while the dog escaped and ripped around the apartment like a terrorist. She heard glass breaking. Finally, after the dog had run himself out, she stole out of the kitchen and hooked a leash to his collar. He followed her into the van like a lamb, nose bloodied. This was just how he acted.

To her eternal surprise, a surprise so profound she fancied it a blessing from on high, Ronny's van started on the first try. She headed south, admiring the view—something she did when alone, which was seldom, now that she thought about it; Devin rarely let her out of his sight. And though he liked her band outfits—little leather vests over spandex tops and black leggings—he didn't like her talking to the misfits who packed into Lester's every night.

Most of them were in their twenties and thirties; Lester's was the "young" bar, as opposed to the "married" bar on the next corner where they played old Eagles tunes, and the "cirrhosis" bar on the corner after that, where Merle Haggard was king.

The veterinary clinic was just north of Homer on Route 1, in a clearing backdropped by a surreal slab of mountain and Cook Inlet. The building looked homey, steeply gabled and painted white, with an attached Cape-style house where a flower garden probably resided beneath the mounting snowdrifts. She got out, the dog springing behind her so aggressively that she lost purchase on her shoes and splatted forward, and then the dog, whining and snapping, stamped all over her in what she construed as a deliberate show of might as she turned her head into the snow, fearing she might drown before she got the damn dog as far as the front door. "Stop it! Stop it!" she shrieked, and the dog went into one his eerie calms. He just sat there. "Good boy," she soothed, "good boy, good boy, good boy," getting up and brushing herself off. She'd broken a strap on her left shoe, and her sleeping-bag coat now had a long tear where the zipper ended.

There was no receptionist. She tied the dog to a chair, close, using a knot—a clove hitch—that her grandfather, ex-Navy, had once showed her. She didn't know why this knot arrived now, in this place, except that her grandparents were on her mind. It seemed to be another sign; of what, she did not know, but there was an odd comfort in this small competence until the dog got up and bumped around the lobby dragging the chair.

The veterinarian, a sweet-looking man with small

bones and dandelion hair, came into the lobby. "Sorry," he said. "Short-handed." He looked her over, not lasciviously, but the way a father might. She sat down and wept openly, not caring what her face must look like, what this nice man must think. He'd seen worse, was her hope. She certainly had.

"It can't be that bad," he said. "You friend here looks saveable." The dog had quieted again, quaking.

She shook her head. "It's not the dog. It's my life."

He blushed, then stood there a moment longer. "Well," he said finally, "does the dog have a name?"

"No," she said, embarrassed. Devin and K.C. had named it something obscene. "I think it might have epilepsy or something."

"Come on back," the vet said, and he held out an arm as if holding a door, allowing her to go ahead of him.

The dog was good, for a few minutes. He submitted to a weigh-in. He let the vet look in his mouth, daub the blood off his nose, feel around under his tummy, check his ears, his eyes, his coat. Then the dog bared his teeth, whipped around, and snapped hard just as the vet pulled back his hand. "Hold on, hold on, pal," the vet said, very calmly, considering that Carrie was still weeping and the dog was winding up for a doozy.

"This your first dog, Miss Whitten?" he asked.

She nodded. "He deserves better than us. He's cooped up in a dark apartment most of the day and all of the night. He's bitten a couple of people, not that I blame him in one case." She looked at the dog, who was doing that swallowy thing that usually preceded an episode.

"I thought maybe you could give him some Prozac or something."

"Let me take him out back," he said. "Then we can talk." He eased the dog out of the room and closed the door. Carrie climbed onto the metal examining table, collapsed, and closed her eyes.

Within minutes the vet was back. He said, "We have chairs."

"I'm up here with a band," she said, staring at the ceiling. "We're playing Lester's in Bryce, waiting for something to open up in Anchorage." She drove the heels of her hands hard under her eyes, hoping he wouldn't ask the band's name. "I'm the singer," she added. "I sing."

"How did you come by this dog?"

"My boyfriend picked him up at a rest stop. He was just wandering around." She sat up, ashamed, moving awkwardly with her oversized coat. "We've been carting him around in a van. It's not what you'd call a stable lifestyle." She thought of the vet's house next door. Probably there was a wife over there, a schoolteacher, maybe. And a little daughter or son.

"It's not actually a dog," the vet informed her. "It's a wolf hybrid. You see that once in a while up here. People find they can't handle them and just let them loose."

Devin would love this. He would just love it. He would write a song about it, and she would have to do the wolfy, howly part while Keith stomped up and down on the distortion pedal.

"You picked a very challenging pet," the vet said.

She slid off the table. "Tell me something I don't know."

"They're not strictly legal," he said earnestly. "Depends on percentages."

"I can't keep him, anyway," she said. "I'm afraid of him. I'm afraid of everything." The vet seemed very kindly, and interested, so she went on: "I'm afraid I won't be able to save enough for a plane ticket out of this place. You wouldn't believe what I get paid, and everything up here's so expensive."

The vet looked at her for a long, embarrassing moment. "I've got an arrangement with a shelter in Anchorage," he said. "It's possible I could find the animal something more—suited."

"I wouldn't have let him loose," Carrie said. "I'm not that bad of a person."

The vet patted her shoulder. "You're a very nice person, Miss Whitten. You've done the right thing for your pet." It sounded like a speech, but she appreciated it anyway. It had been months, maybe even years, since somebody told her she had done something right.

"Thank you," she said. "I think I'm pregnant."

He blushed again—she found it endearing, and he made her feel older, somehow, as if she had to teach him how to act around a person like her. "I can't help you on that score, I'm afraid," he said.

"I just wondered if you might have something around here—" She was looking directly into a little cubby stocked with bottles of pills. "I mean, like a morning-after pill, something that you use on animals, but maybe on a person—"

He held up his hands. "There's nothing like that. I'm

sorry." He ushered her back out to the lobby, but she couldn't leave.

"You said you were shorthanded, right?" She had her life planned again, all of a sudden. She would work as this lovely man's receptionist, and take a room in his cozy house, which probably looked a lot like her room at home, with the daisy wallpaper her mother had picked out for her when she was nine years old and too young to know better, and she could just hang out here, interviewing people who might want to adopt a wolf-dog, and for a little extra pay she could babysit their adorable little daughter, who would probably be impressed as hell that Carrie was, or had been, a singer in a band, and would love the little-girl things Carrie brought her, like sparkles and Barbie clothes. She'd have her baby and stay on as a receptionist-nanny and never have to face her parents with such an obvious, predictable failure.

"My assistant's down with the flu," he said. "She'll be back tomorrow. I'm sorry." Now he looked afraid of her, more afraid than he'd seemed around the dog, who bit and snapped and was part wolf and God Almighty did she look that bad? Did she look like some hybrid thing that was too much to take on?

"Should I pay you?" she managed.

"No," he said. "It's all right. Maybe you should call your mother."

Back in the van, she saw that she did look like some hybrid thing, loosely strung and scary. She wiped her face with the sleeve of her sleeping-bag coat, leaving makeup smears along the cuff. She sat in the van for a long time, then, in the perpetual dusk, drove north to Bryce. She stopped once, at a gas station, to get a latte—this godforsaken middle-of-nowhere was lousy with good coffee—and headed back, for lack of a better word, home. Devin was tipping back a whiskey sour, an old-man drink. K.C., Milo, and some girl they'd picked up were passing around a joint—hash, from the smell of it. This place was full of throwback drugs.

"How is he?" Devin asked. He gave her a long, sloppy kiss, whacked out of his mind; she was in for a long afternoon.

"He might have epilepsy," she said. "They're giving him a brain X-ray or something. I gave the guy all hundred-fifty, but it might end up being more."

"Easy come, easy go," Devin said, pulling her into the bedroom. He laid her down and stroked her hair. "What happened to your face?" he asked.

"I fell," she said. She watched him take his shirt off. "Then the dog walked all over me."

"What's this?" he said, lifting her wrist, squinting at the number scrawled across the back of her hand.

"My grandmother died," she said. "I'm grieving." She turned over on the bed and hid her face. She felt the bed move, a hand on her calf. Then a cool trail of sensation as the hand moved up the back of her thigh. She began to weep: big, man-sized hiccups that shook the blankets. She felt him hovering for a moment, heard his black-lunged breathing; then he crept out and closed the door, leaving her in blessed silence until it was time to leave for the gig.

The crowd that night was a good one, from Lester's point of view: drinking a lot, dancing, using the pool tables to actually play pool. The first set included five of Devin's own tunes plus their signature cover of "Anarchy in the U.K." by the Sex Pistols. Every time Carrie grabbed the mic, her grandfather's phone number appeared in front of her, augmented by her clenched fist. At the break she went downstairs to throw up in the ladies' room, then stopped at the pay phone and stuck her card in.

When her grandfather's voice came on the phone, groggy and grief-stricken, she realized, in horror, that it was the middle of the night in Maine. "It's Carrie, Grampa," she said. "I just realized about the time."

"I was awake," he said. She got a terrible picture of him standing in his underwear, the house dark and bare, his bed empty.

"I'm sorry about Grandma," she said. She put one hand over her ear to hear him better. The jukebox above her head sounded muffled and throbbing, like a heart struggling its last.

"Where are you?" her grandfather asked.

"In Alaska. I'm in a band. I'm between sets right now."

She heard a terrible chuffing sound and realized he was weeping. She waited, aware of the minutes draining off her phone card.

"Did Mom and Dad get there yet?" she asked.

"Tomorrow," he said, after another awful silence.

"Did you get your job back, Grampa?" she asked hopefully.

"Looks like a long haul on that score. Thirteen months

and holding." He blew his nose. "Sing one for your grand-mother, dear, would you? She loved music."

Because that one word, *dear*, so wholesome and old-fashioned, reached her like a warm breath, she could not manage another word, and before she could wrack out a simple goodbye, the phone line blinked off and she was out of time.

First up was "Summertime." Carrie clambered onto the stage, where someone had dropped a wet hamburger bun. She knocked it away with her foot, still encased in her new shoes despite the broken strap.

"You watch yourself," Devin warned as he strapped on his guitar, a Strat with gold pegs that he traded off with a Les Paul Flame Top that could bring in enough money at auction to buy a small country. His eyes looked like broken plates.

She straightened up. "It's mine."

"You can sing any fucking thing you want after you've paid you're dues." His voice went slurry and numb-sound-ing. They would have to carry him home. "You pay your dues first," he said, "then you come back to me with this lullaby bullshit."

Carrie took a step toward him, surprised to discover that in her new shoes she could face him nose to nose. "You want to talk about dues? How about being old, and you have to actually work for a living, and the mill goes on strike for a year, and then your wife dies, and your bed's empty in the middle of the night for the first time in like forty years? That's paying your dues, my friend."

Ronny flipped the power switch. A single shriek issued from the speakers as Carrie snatched the mic off its stand. The place went quiet, then a burble of laughter erupted from the vicinity of the pool table. K.C. banged out the opening bars with the fuzzbox right on tilt. Devin muttered, "Just sing it," clenching the whang bar on his Stratocaster as if it were Carrie's neck. Milo crashed in with the drums a measure late, Keith and Ronny came in on bass and rhythm guitar more or less on time, and Toxic Scream erupted into full thrash mode, a shatter of sound and fury signifying absolutely nothing, but they got the place jumping before Carrie could get in a note.

She opened her mouth. *Summertime,* she sang, *and the livin' is easy.* She placed the mic in its stand, put two graceful fingers to her ears, listening only to the inside of her head, singing each note deliberately, a swoon of sound far beneath the noise of the band, and though she was several bars behind now and counting, she did not give in, she had three fifties in her pocket, it was a start, and in the meantime she would not give in, she wouldn't, she would see this song through, straight through, singing in her old way, as if her one purpose in being born had been to sing somebody to sleep.

The Joy Business

CINDY LOVE, *proprietor,*
Showers of Flowers

S ix days after Cindy's first divorce, the door to her flower shop jangled opened and in walked another man. He wanted flowers, he said. Help me.

"For your wife?" Cindy asked.

He laughed. "Hardly." He drummed his long, ringless, privileged-looking fingers on Cindy's counter. "Tenure party," he said, making the words sound dull and obligational, but to Cindy they had a different tang altogether. The college, only forty minutes away by car, occupied a world rarely felt here.

Bruce Love was his name. He taught studio art, he told her, though he himself was a sculptor. Beautiful teeth, an artistic nose, a shiver of well-cut hair. She recommended something showy—bird of paradise, stargazer lilies—and he went for it, watching as she added lobelia and baby's breath, wrapping the bouquet in tissue so fine it could line a bird's nest.

When she was finished, Bruce Love asked if she might

consider delivering the flowers in person, as his date. Love to, she said, ringing up his order, her ten childless years as Mrs. Danny Little dropping away behind her, drifty as rose petals. His wallet contained pictures of children, a boy and a girl. His check showed that he lived here, in Abbott Falls, only blocks from where she'd moved back in with her mother. She envisioned a long, glamorous string of tenure parties—plus free courses at the college and two brilliant stepchildren who adored her—waiting at the misty end of the evening. Yes indeed, she said. Tonight. You bet.

THE PARTY unfolded in excruciating flats of time, like acts in a bad play. At one point Don Pratt, the party's host, hauled up from his cellar six bottles of old wine. He poured the first glass for his wife, Ann Pratt, in honor of her bitterly gotten tenure. There were twenty guests, including an English professor with tiny eyes named Barnes Parke or Parke Barnes, and his girlfriend, also a professor, with the first name of Marina and a last name that sounded like *Perestroika* but couldn't be. The others were introduced so rapidly Cindy couldn't remember even one of them, though she prided herself on her good memory. The evening became more theatrical as it wore on, with smart people drifting in and out of doorways, trailing ribbons of perfectly timed one-liners and intelligent-sounding laughter. The wine smelled vaguely of dirt. Cindy left most of it—about fifty dollars' worth, she guessed—sitting in her glass.

"Leave it to Bruce to walk in for flowers and walk out with the florist," Don Pratt said suddenly. There was something aggressive in his long, thin smile.

"That's our Bruce," said a woman in spaghetti straps who had been introduced to Cindy as a "fellow." She raised her glass in an ambiguous toast.

"Do not get your hopes up," added Marina Perestroika, in her heavy, alluring accent. "Bruce is the ladies' men." An edgy murmur of laughter followed.

"They're all drunk," Bruce laughed, sliding his arm over Cindy's shoulders. "Don't listen."

Cindy opened her mouth to say something, but Parke or Barnes leapt in with a joke she didn't get, and they were off and running without her.

Cindy, however, was no fool. The instant the words "tenure party" had escaped Bruce Love's beautiful lips, she'd taken him for a man uneasy in his skin. Five minutes in this house had revealed to her how much he disliked his colleagues. She understood that Bruce had brought her here to play the working-class gal in the flared skirt—she'd seen enough movies. And she didn't mind being flaunted. Cindy planned to woo Bruce Love by playing her part beyond his expectations. She planned to tell the story of her flower shop, Showers of Flowers, how everyone in her ex-husband's family said she couldn't do it, she with no head for numbers. She planned for someone to squeal, "Isn't that just the most *darling* name for a shop!" and ask her opinion on a houseplant they couldn't keep alive.

She did not plan to feel overlooked and outclassed.

But there it was. More than half the guests drifted out the door without so much as catching Cindy's name.

Then: "I've got something *fun*," Ann Pratt said, getting up and carrying her wine into the den. Her husband, following her, rolled his eyes and said, "She's hooked on that infernal game," and the remaining guests, following Don, said, "What game?" except for Cindy, who noticed, with the relief of a drowning victim, a flame-orange box floating on the glass top of Ann and Don Pratt's coffee table. The box housed two stacks of four-inch-square cards containing riddles, conundrums, word puzzles, twisters of every stripe. "MindMelt," Cindy said, pretending to read the box. "Huh."

"Boys against girls," Ann gushed, moving people into chairs.

"This is *so* Ann," Bruce whispered into Cindy's ear. "You want to go?"

"No," Cindy said. "I want to stay." Bruce looked nervous. She wondered whether he feared his own humiliation, or hers; either way it endeared him to her.

Parke-or-Barnes selected a card and read: "Question: If your house is freezing and you have a kerosene lamp, six candles, and a coal stove, what should you light first?"

Ann, Marina, and the Fellow conferred frantically.

"Time!" the men shouted.

Cindy said quietly, "A match." Everyone looked at her. She shrugged prettily. "You light a match."

There was a pause. Oh, for God's sake, the women groaned, how could we have *missed* it, it was so *obvious*, so *easy*, hooray for Cindy!

Bruce looked at her. She snapped her eyes away, possessed of a secret.

The ladies kept their turn.

Don read this time: "Question: How did the hiker get killed by the pack on his back?"

Cindy sat by as the women mulled some ridiculous possibilities. "It's a trick question," Ann fretted.

The men were laughing. Bruce was laughing, too, and for a moment, as he leaned back in Don Pratt's tapestried love seat, one leg crossing over the other, he looked exactly, exactly like Don Pratt, until he caught Cindy looking at him and shifted position, his elbows crashing down on his knees, wineglass gripped like a beer mug between his hands.

Don flipped the card over, snorted, and said, "They'll never get it."

But Cindy knew the answer. She knew all the answers, and felt a penetrating jolt of gratitude toward her ex-husband. As a couple they had suffered a string of disappointments both vague and obvious, odd eruptions of mutual blaming, and finally a long, difficult parting. She was glad for all of it now. Danny's family—a chummy band of millworkers and their kids—had played endless rounds of MindMelt on Friday nights, teams arranged and rearranged, running tallies posted in all the kitchens. Once they'd exhausted all five hundred cards, they transformed it from a game of knowledge to a game of memory.

And thank God, Cindy thought. Thank God for those Friday nights.

"It's not a backpack," she said. "It's a pack of wolves."

"By gum, she's right again," Don said, just like a professor in a play. He grabbed another card: "How far can a dog run into the Lincoln Tunnel?"

Ann frowned. "What kind of question is that?"

"Halfway," Cindy offered calmly. "After that, the dog would be running *out* of the Lincoln Tunnel."

The women gaped at her. The men were beginning to sulk.

On the next few questions Cindy allowed her teammates a few foolish guesses, and then she didn't, spitting out the right answers like *that*, like *that*, like *that*, until Bruce turned square around, bestowing upon her his full and frank attention.

Surprise, she said with her eyes. I'm good at games.

IF ALL had gone well in the three years after the wedding, if she had set out on the stimulating trail she'd imagined on that first day, Cindy might have carved out a moment in which to confess the tiny fraud she'd perpetrated at the home of Don and Ann Pratt. But Bruce was not above a little fraud of his own, as it turned out. He had nothing saved. He had not sold a piece in five years. He had yet to get tenure. She found a note to a female student that could be taken more than one way. She saw another move in his future, another divorce in hers. This knowledge muted the days, but she had children to think of now: a girl named Francine who regarded her as if she'd floated in on Glinda the Good Witch's bubble, and Francine's older brother, Kenny, who Cindy believed would just as soon have dropped a house on her.

She spent her happiest hours at the shop with Francine, who joined her after school, stocking the cooler and recording invoices while Cindy manned the counter. Cindy was teaching Francine to arrange poinsettia baskets when the call came. It was Bruce, with an invitation from Ann and Don Pratt.

"Remember that stupid game?" he said. "Mindsweeper or something? The new version's out and they're looking for a rematch." He laughed. "Couple against couple, Ann says. This is war, baby."

Cindy smiled. These intermittent moments she called intimacy felt like a series of dots that might still connect into a picture that made sense. He took a noisy sip of something: she pictured him in his small office adjacent to the art studios, drinking coffee. Who else was there? Who else waiting? "Shouldn't we let them win?" she asked hopefully.

Something in the air hovered disagreeably; Don Pratt was on Bruce's tenure review committee. "Fuck, no," Bruce said. "We bury the bastards." She could hear an arty-sounding commotion in the background, easels being put up or taken down. "I need you, babe. I need my girl with the answers."

But Cindy was out of answers. She hung up and glanced around the shop. "Francine," she said, "do you think you could hold the fort? I have to run out for a minute."

Francine—a myopic, unlovely eighth-grader—brightened, her hand on the phone. "If a really big order comes in, can I take it?"

Cindy shrugged on her parka and swung her purse from a hook. "You can sell the place if you get a good enough offer."

"I'd never do that," Francine said, shocked. Then: "Oh. A joke."

Cindy sighed. Francine, who was whip-smart and better than any of the part-timers Cindy had hired and fired over the years, had been born with absolutely no sense of irony. Her adoration, guileless and unconditional, made Cindy feel too powerful most of the time, an irony she could barely stand to contemplate.

Two hours later, after panicking through Woolworth's, Flint's, Rite-Aid, and the strip mall on Libby Road, Cindy pulled back in front of her shop empty-handed. As she sat in the cold car considering her options—there had to be a MindMelt II somewhere in this town, there had to be—she spotted her ex-husband, Danny Little, coming down the sidewalk with a yellow dog.

She felt extravagantly glad to see him, someone who had known her before she'd been granted the wish of a different life. "You got a dog," she said, getting out of the car.

"Your replacement," he said, not bitterly. "How's life on College Row?"

"We never moved." She lifted her chin toward the shop. "You should stop in once in a while, you'd know these things." Since the divorce, Danny and his entire family had managed to avoid her altogether.

"I'm not much in the market for flowers," he said.

"Nobody is," she admitted. The mill had been on strike for ten months now. She'd seen Danny on television the night before, caught on the slushy picket line with his face scrunched up like a tin can, wielding a crowbar and spitting onto the greasy window of a pickup during shift change.

"I saw the news," she said softly. "Dan, I barely recognized you."

His eyes flickered. "You're not the only one." Now he held her gaze. "Timmy crossed."

Timmy was the youngest of all those brothers, his favorite. "Crossed?" Cindy said, half-comprehending. "You mean the picket line?"

Danny nodded, his face puffy with grief. She found that she could still read him like a wife: he had given his brother up.

"Danny, I don't believe you." She was of the opinion that love made exceptions to life's most exacting rules. He looked haggard and old, and perhaps she alone was able to understand how much this breach had cost him. Thick as thieves, she used to think of them, thick as thieves, the flypaper family.

Cindy scanned the weathering town, its snowy hills gone ash-colored in the overcast afternoon. "Maybe it will end soon." She imagined herself as a striker's wife, collecting cans for the food bank.

"Is that your stepdaughter?" Danny asked.

Cindy nodded. Francine was waving mightily from the display window, where she was lining up the flower baskets, placing them into military rows. Her big sweat-shirt read SCABS OUT! UNION IN!

"I've seen her down at the union hall," Danny said.

"She's been volunteering," Cindy told him. Francine was tapping on the glass now, gesturing toward a display that Cindy would have to do over. After Cindy gave the thumbs-up, Francine climbed out of the window, lowering one lumbery leg at a time. Embarrassed, Cindy glanced away. "She was four when their mother left," Cindy sighed. "She follows me like a dog."

"Seems like a nice kid."

"She is," Cindy said. "Smart, too. Scary-smart. She's designing my Web site."

"You mean on the Internet?"

Cindy smiled wearily. "She's planning to make me rich."

He was looking at her as if to say, *You're trusting a kid with your future?* Which was a good point, an excellent point, but she'd hitched her wagon to dimmer stars than this.

"Listen," she said. "I'm sorry about Tim."

"Yeah," he said. "He's gone now, anyway. Off to parts unknown. I thought you'd want to know." He bent to adjust something on the dog's collar. It was a sweet dog, well-mannered. We should have had a dog, she thought.

"Anyway," Danny said. "I'm glad you finally got the kids you wanted."

"They're not the kids I wanted," Cindy said. In a rush of regret and nostalgia, she blundered toward her former husband and his arms came around her. They stood that way for a very long moment, long enough so that she began to remember what it was like to be held by him before they'd been worn apart by their respective sorrows.

Francine was watching, of course, but Cindy didn't mind. Her stepdaughter had been observing this town like a historian for months now, and she seemed to understand better than Cindy that all the rules of protocol had changed. Francine had once witnessed two women— one a striker, one a strikebreaker's wife—leap out of their cars to slap each other's face, then reported it to Cindy with the composure of a war correspondent.

Danny's dog began to tug on its leash. Cindy blurted, "Remember that game?" and before she knew what she was doing she had confessed her three-year-old con. Danny chuckled a little, shaking his head. His old face flashed out from the blotched, grieving one, and she was glad she had told him just for that, for a two-second glimpse of her old life.

"Oh, God, Danny," she said. "Don't tell anyone."

"I won't." Their breath mingled in tiny, cold clouds.

"Especially not your family, Danny. Really." She stopped. "Listen, you don't, you don't happen to have a copy of the new MindMelt that I could borrow?"

He looked at her. "We don't play anymore. Cindy, we don't even talk."

There had been a time when the Littles' not talking would have been her dearest wish. But now she retreated into her shop, aware of Francine's appraising eyes. Danny's family, so fastened by blood and history, had been in love with themselves as a unit, a secret club, a gravitational force. If a family like that could collapse at this late stage, then what hope was there for hers?

THAT NIGHT'S supper was a typical one in the Love household: Kenny gulping his food, holding his plate away from the table as if the lot of them had rabies; Bruce making painful small talk with Francine about her day at school; Cindy turning out radish curls that nobody noticed except Francine, who noticed everything.

"Wasn't that your ex-husband today?" Kenny asked.

Bruce looked up. Then Francine.

"I was coming out of the VideoMart," Kenny explained, the soul of innocence. "Looked like a deep conversation."

"He's having a bad time," Cindy said evenly. She nibbled at a glazed carrot, having learned early on to give Kenny's assaults more room than they required. "I've actually thought about sending him flowers, but I wouldn't want him to take it the wrong way."

"What other way is there to take it?" Bruce said.

Francine stopped chewing. "I can think of at least twelve."

But Bruce was getting up, acting the wounded husband, an act that Cindy recognized as the righteous indignation of a sinner. She caught a glimpse of his face as he turned from the table, his eyes fixed in the middle distance, where the student he was screwing floated hotly, half in and half out of her paint-smattered shirt, her pinkish breasts turned up and asking.

Kenny pushed his plate back. "You're a sculptor, Dad," he said, switching to his true target, his voice well aimed and soft with condescension. "Cindy dumped the guy for you. What's to worry?"

"You've got your facts out of order, Kenny," Cindy said, mortified. Was this what everybody thought? Was this what Danny thought?

"Kenny always has his facts out of order," Bruce said, turning around. "Which is just the damnedest thing for a kid who knows everything."

Kenny scraped his chair back—a hard scrape that changed the tenor of the room. "Then let's do it, Dad," he said, staring his father down. "Let's put the facts in order. What do you say, Dad? Want to put the facts in order?"

Cindy held her breath, sensing a plate-rattling showdown in the works, a bad one, a naming of names, a litany of things Kenny knew about his father that Cindy did not want Francine to hear. But Bruce apparently had other plans. Before Kenny could wind himself up another notch, Bruce had slammed out the door and his car was spitting up ice as he screeched into the street. Kenny slipped into his room, eerily wordless, leaving Francine and Cindy and a glory of leftovers.

Cindy remained where she was, Francine silent across from her, until the sound of Bruce's car faded far around the corner. She waited for the air to settle, for the kitchen clock to take over the management of time. Then she took up her fork, and Francine did likewise. They finished eating.

"I like what you put on the carrots," Francine said.

Cindy thanked her. Then: "I didn't leave one man for another, Francine. I would never do that."

"I know you wouldn't," Francine said solemnly. "Kenny's a jerk." She took up some plates and put them in the sink. "You want to see what I'm working on?"

Cindy followed Francine to her room. This is what her evenings came to. She sat patiently, the way she had so many times since she had become Francine's default mother. Bruce's first wife had moved to London and showed no signs of ever coming back. The photograph on Francine's desk hadn't been updated in years, so it was impossible to know what she looked like now, but Cindy felt a profound, unwanted kinship with this woman who knew what it was like to be Mrs. Bruce Love: that peculiar loneliness, the kind that intensified the nearer he got.

"Watch this," Francine said, presenting a scanned image of Cindy on the computer screen. The image startled her. She looked like a movie star holding flowers so vivid you wanted to eat them. A little flutter happened inside her, a feeling like, God help her, a bud opening. She thought, I'd buy flowers from her. I'd buy anything from her.

"How'd you do that?" Cindy asked.

Francine grinned. "Magic."

From downstairs came the sound of Kenny slamming out of the house, then the more distant *rrr-rrr-rrr* of Cindy's car struggling to start in the cold.

"He didn't even ask you," Francine said. "I don't like him anymore." Finally the engine turned over, and Cindy relaxed.

"When I was little he used to ride me around on his handlebars," Francine said. "I was his favorite little kid of all time."

Cindy did not know how to answer this.

Francine shook her head—gravely, as if presiding over a death. Cindy thought something might be wrong with the computer, until Francine blurted, "He's leaving. I know it."

Cindy touched Francine's hair, which was coarse and old-feeling. "Well, he'll graduate soon," she said.

"No," Francine muttered. "That's not what I meant. He's already gone, really." She hunched over the keyboard, blinking hard, clicking here and there. "A lady came into the shop today while you were out," she said. "She wanted two dozen roses with the buds cut off. Just the sticks, that's all. She wanted to send her brother a big bunch of thorny dead sticks." She stared at the screen. "They're on opposite sides."

"What did you say to her?" Cindy asked.

Francine looked up; Cindy received her face in all its homely beauty. "I told her we were in the joy business."

She clicked the keyboard again and another image showed up: an order form accompanied by a different photograph, a long shot that Cindy couldn't place. She'd been caught outside the shop in summer, her back to the camera, hanging a basket of fuchsia, midday sunshine showering over her glinting hair. The real surprise was the town, which looked green and prosperous: window boxes brimming, doors flung wide, open flags rippling. You could tell everyone was working.

"Where'd you get this?" Cindy asked, squinting at the screen.

"I took it."

"When?"

Francine hesitated. "Last summer, I think. It was last summer."

"That's not last summer, honey," Cindy said slowly. "That's, what, four years ago, at least."

Francine shook her head.

Now Cindy got serious. "I replaced that plant hanger a long time ago, Francine. When did you take this?"

Francine sat back, her skin blotching. "Before Dad knew you," she admitted.

Cindy regarded Francine, accosted by a deep unease. "Why would you have taken my picture before Dad knew me?"

Francine cast her eyes down, the pale lashes fluttering behind her thick glasses. "I don't know. I picked you out. I told him and told him. Once I came in the shop just to look at you close." She was crying a little, and Cindy hardly knew what to do. She was too shocked to be angry; she couldn't imagine Francine, who would have been nine years old back then, roaming the streets of Abbott Falls looking for a mother.

"Kenny's leaving," Francine was saying, not looking at anything but the image on the screen. "Don't you leave us, too." She passed a pudgy palm across her handiwork, which now looked desperate with effort. "You can't leave. I'm going to make you rich."

"You don't have to make me rich, Francine," Cindy whispered. "I'm not going anywhere." You can say *that* again, said a voice in the back of her head. Then she stroked the scratchy hair of this child who loved flowers.

"Did that woman say something to you today, Francine?" Cindy asked. "The dead-sticks lady?"

"No," Francine said. "It's not that." She sighed like an old woman. "She just went away. I tried to explain, but she wasn't listening. Nobody in this town is listening."

AFTER FRANCINE went to bed, Cindy sat up in the dark living room. Bruce, as usual, wasn't home. Something at the college, an awards dinner or seminar or colloquium. Or.

She heard her car pull up around midnight—that telltale whir—and Kenny sauntered in. Most boys his age would be red-faced and reeking, but Kenny seemed composed, as if he'd spent the evening discussing math theorems or sitting alone in a diner.

"Where's your husband?" he asked. In his voice she detected a note of resignation that moved her unaccountably. She wondered if what she had taken for scorn all these years had been something else altogether: pity, perhaps. He looked older to her, at this hour, in this room, in this quiet.

Cindy got up, facing him. "That's not your car," she informed him.

Kenny was all angles, both inside and out, but in his layered eyes resided something worn-looking, too bowed for a boy his age. "I'm going to bed," he said. "Francine all right?"

"Of course she's all right," Cindy said. "Why wouldn't she be?"

He shrugged. "It's a terrible world."

"No, it isn't, Kenny."

"No?"

"No," she said. "It's not a terrible world. And ask permission next time."

He observed her for a long, uncomfortable moment. She felt judged, but not harshly. "I can't believe you're still here," he murmured. "Nobody else would be."

Then he went off to bed, and by the time Bruce arrived—*he* was red-faced and reeking—she had prepared and discarded a goodbye speech and simply told him, standing at the doorway in her blue bathrobe, "I'm staying, Bruce. I will not abandon the children."

He stood in front of her, weaving a little, looking raffish, irresponsible—exactly like the sort of man she would have fallen for had she gone to college herself. She knew this, and forgave the girl, whoever she was, forgave her stupidity, her yawning need to feel necessary.

"Hey," he said, caressing her shoulders. "What's this? What's this we're talking about?"

She leveled him with a look, feeling glassy and tall. She tried to picture him as he would look a few days hence, installed in a comfortable chair at the home of Don and Ann Pratt, realizing at this late date that he'd married a woman unskilled at riddles. "Francine needs me," she said. "Kenny can do without, he's done without, he knows how. But Francine, Francine found me, and here I am, and I insist"—she said *insist* like the character in the play she'd been in now for three years—"I *insist* that you behave better, Bruce, I won't stand for this."

He gave her a woozy smile. "I can't imagine what you're talking about," he said, then opened the front of her robe as if parting curtains. She gave him a shove, stomped out to the porch, and stood shivering under the stars for as long as she could stand it. The sky shone clearer these days, the mill smoke having thinned in the strike's long wake. Production was down. The nightly gauntlet—the banging and shouting, the flashing lights, the signs being raised and lowered like pistons—was too distant to hear, though she strained to hear it, that desperate desire to take back, reclaim, salvage, repossess. Perhaps the picketers had quit for the night, Danny and his brothers and the rest of the displaced having already shut their separate doors, leaving the town to this shocking stillness. She would see Francine through high school. She believed she could do at least that. She sensed the dull, pleasant town of her childhood as a recognizable entity somewhere just beyond reach, as still and poignant as a dead animal, beautiful and beyond revival.

Visitors

JAMES WHITTEN, *software consultant*

When James arrived at Karen's new apartment, he could not help but note how young she looked, how honeyed and golden, as if to prove her contention that divorcing a man like James Whitten would take years off a sane woman's face.

"What do you want?" she asked, politely enough.

"My mother died."

The sweet folds near her mouth softened, making her look, suddenly, her age, which was forty-five, two years older than he was. "Oh," she sighed, letting him in. "I'm sorry, Jamie. When?"

"Last night," he said, moving into the polished light of Karen's bay window, from which he could just make out the artful curve of the Golden Gate Bridge. "My father called me."

She guided him to a chair, then sat across from him, knee to knee. "Your mother was a brave woman."

"I bought two plane tickets," he said. "I was hoping you'd come with me."

"Of course I'll come," she said. "Why wouldn't I come?"

"Because you hate me."

"I don't hate you, Jamie," she said gently. "It's just that I'm not suffering as much as we thought I would." She lifted her head. "Did you think to call Carrie?"

He said nothing.

Karen swiped a hand through her hair—recently shorn, boyish and sexy—a gesture he recognized as irritation. "Do you even have her number?"

"An old one," he said. "Who the hell can keep track?"

"I'll call," Karen said, getting up. She whisked into the bedroom, where he overheard enough to reassure himself that despite her denials, Karen shared his disgust at their daughter's latest caper: singing in some Alaskan bar with her smug, pretty-boy, guitar-smashing boyfriend. He went to the doorway of her bedroom, where she was just hanging up. "She claims she'll call her grandfather," Karen said, "but she won't." She flicked the briefest glance at James—*chip off the old block*—then hauled a suitcase out of the closet and threw it on the bed.

"There's something you should know," he said.

She sat on the edge of the bed and looked at him. "Let me guess," she said, her lips drawing into a predictable line. "You didn't tell them about the divorce."

He shook his head.

"And I suppose you were thinking, good old Karen, she'll come to the funeral, make everything comfy, and then drop an oh-by-the-way as we're getting back on the plane."

"Something like that," he admitted.

She snapped open the suitcase and dropped some underwear inside. "You said you'd tell them, Jamie."

"Well, I didn't." He looked at the floor. He'd been hoping for a little more in the way of sympathy. "What difference does it make?" he asked. "You would have come anyway."

"Not as your wife."

"Technically, you still are," he said.

Her eyes held him evenly. "Ten more days."

He lifted his arms, a gesture reminiscent of a thief showing his empty pockets. "You were her daughter-in-law for nineteen years, Karen," he said, fearful that she might change her mind. "You ought to be there."

She stood up, her leggings bunched at the knees, making her look like a child at a parade. "Yes," she quavered. "You bet I ought to be there. Marie was the soul of sweetness. God, I was going to call her this week. *Yesterday* I was going to call her, and I didn't. I had the damn *phone* in my *lap*, and I didn't." She drove her hands across her eyes, smearing her makeup. It was Karen who had called his mother after every round of her tests, Karen who sent bed jackets and bath beads even as they fought in a therapist's office once a week and prepped their finances for the big breach.

"Your mother was an angel," she went on, swiping a black dress off a hanger. "I'll never forgive myself." She added a small tumble of clothing, a few cosmetics, a pair of shoes. Then she took off her shirt, stripped off her leggings, and found a skirt and a silk blouse, a purple one he'd always liked. Karen was the only person he knew who still dressed up for plane rides.

"I was waiting for you to tell them, Jamie. I was so sick of pretending we were still together. I haven't called once in *three* weeks. Her three *final* weeks, it now turns out. I was waiting you out, because you *said* you'd tell them, and now it's too late." She stopped abruptly, turning to him, a bra he'd never seen catching the light in a soul-filling twin flash. "Do you *mind*?"

James turned around, the view out her bedroom door considerably less inspiring. Her place was all hardwood and white walls and airy furniture, the opposite of the stolid furniture she'd filled their life with over the years. He was stuck with it now, all that weight. In the end it was she who had left.

"I wanted her to die not knowing," he said after a while.

"How considerate," she muttered. She was referring to his parents' visits to California over the years, James always busy with work, leaving Karen and Carrie to take them around, chat on the deck, ride the cable cars. He had not been a considerate son.

"Turn around," she said. He did. Fully dressed, she stood with her arms crossed, head cocked as if listening for alarms. "You know why I'm doing this?"

"Because you like my parents," he said. He had said this before.

"Do you know *why* I like your parents, Jamie?" she said, the thin cords of her neck pulsing.

James tried to look calm, unirritated: he needed her.

"Because they keep your name by the phone," he recited. "They remember your birthday. They show more interest in you from three thousand miles away than I ever did from across the table."

She made a low, anguished groan, which reminded him uncomfortably of sex. With her. "They're in *love*," she said, swinging the packed case off the bed. "That's why I like them. The way they look at each other, after all those years, it makes me want to gouge out my eyes."

Though James agreed that he and Karen had never belonged together, that for nineteen years he had been cold and vague and a distant father and unsuited to the tasks of love, that he was little more than a visitor in his own life, that being James Whitten's wife was a purgatory no woman should be forced to endure, he could still be surprised by her anger. She was at heart a temperate woman.

"Christ," she sighed. She covered her face. "I'm sorry."

"It's all right."

"How is he?"

"Who?"

"Your *father*, Jamie. God."

James said, "All right, I think. He didn't say much." Then, because Karen had always been the keeper of tickets—theater, movie, plane—he handed them to her.

She studied them, frowning. "We're staying one day? With your bereaved father?"

He put his fingers to his temples, his head throbbing. His sports coat felt tight across the back and sadly wrinkled, like a costume for an actor playing the overwrought salesman. "I've got clients lined up around the clock, Karen."

Her eyes—he suspected tinted contacts, another surprise—went liquid and pitying. "You tell them your mother died, Jamie," she said softly. "This is something normal people understand."

Her words hurt. "Are you going to do this all the way to Maine?" he asked.

She shook her head, moving toward him. "No," she said, touching his face, and she meant it, for by the time his father picked them up at the airport in Portland, James felt very nearly married again, Karen in the dark front seat, her head inclined, coaxing a few words from his father, filling the silences between two silent men with her own brand of mercy.

IN THE frigid light of the next morning, James discovered, between the sunporch and the neighbor's fence, a bizarre, shed-sized structure made of wood. Under a shroud of old snow, it resembled a boat, but not quite.

"That's an ark," his father said, trudging out the door. "I built it for your mother."

James exchanged a look with Karen. She said, "I didn't know you were the seafaring type, Ernie."

"It's not for sailing," his father said. "It's for looking at." He turned to James, his lower lids red and sagging. At sixty-five he had passed overnight into old age. "What with the strike lasting a God's age, I had nothing else to do. Your mother likes art."

James followed his father outside, regarding the ark in a mute awe, wondering how Ernie Whitten, a pipefitter on strike, had come to imagine himself an artist between James's last visit and this one. A long time between visits, granted. But still. He passed in front of the ark's strange weight and opened the car door for his father.

The funeral would simply have to be gotten through, James thought; and of course he did get through it, sitting in the front pew next to his father, who remained rigid and mute during the service, no more or less trouble than if he were an armoire James had been consigned to lug around. Karen tended to the mourners, weeping intermittently. In the churchyard it was left to him to drive his father home. As he pulled up to the house, James realized he'd been counting the hours and they were almost up.

A woman stood on the doorstep, waiting. A skeletal, spent-looking woman about James's age, carrying a big beaded purse. She had faded blond hair and a sad, complicated mouth.

"Mr. Whitten?" she asked.

James and his father answered simultaneously: "Yes?"

The woman's eyes rested on Ernie. "I'm Tracey Martin? Used to be Brighton? Tracey Brighton? Back when I—when I met your wife?" Her breath made tiny clouds that James could almost read.

"Thank you for coming," Ernie said. He sounded scraped clean.

"You remember me?" the woman asked, purse rattling as she clutched it to her chest.

Ernie continued through the door, looking exhausted

and benumbed. Not knowing what else to do, James ushered the woman inside. He glanced up the street, hoping to find Karen, who had stayed behind in the icy churchyard to invite people back to the house.

The woman glanced around the foyer, then took a deep breath. "I'm sorry, is what I came to say." Her bony hands shook. "I came all the way up from New London, Connecticut, to say that."

"Thank you," his father said. Then he struggled upstairs as if walking on burned feet.

The woman, Tracey, watched him until he made the landing and disappeared. She gestured vaguely after him, looking confused, then turned to James. "Are you the son?"

"I am," he said. "Look, my wife's bringing some people back. You could have a seat while we wait."

"Oh, if you're having people," she said, looking around frantically. Her purse rattled again. "Look, if I could just have a word with your mother. It won't take long."

"Pardon?" James asked, alarmed. His mother had befriended all kinds over the years.

"Your mother," Tracey said. "Just a word. I have something for her. If she'll see me, that is. Not that I'd blame her, I wouldn't." She placed the purse on a chair as if staking claim, looking directly at James through large, unnervingly blue eyes.

"I don't understand what you mean," James said. His neck felt odd and tingly.

"This *is* the Whitten residence?" she asked. "Marie and Ernest Whitten?"

The front door opened and in walked Karen. Behind her came Alma and Brad Collins, longtime neighbors, carrying groceries. All down the street came the muffled dominos-dropping sound of car doors being opened and then slammed shut.

"Am I in the right place?" Tracey asked, her strange mouth quivering.

"Yes, yes," Karen said. "We'll have things set out in a jiffy." Alma and Brad moved closer into the room, bearing the polite, wounded smiles of the bereaved.

Now Tracey seemed on the verge of tears. She worked at the top button of a too-large coat, a homely blue car coat ill-suited to the December cold. "Where's your mother?" she asked James.

He stared at her. "We've just come from her funeral."

Tracey's hands flew to her face. "Oh! I'm sorry!" She grabbed her big purse. "This is so embarrassing! My God, I've never been so embarrassed!"

Alma and Brad fled to the kitchen. James longed to follow them: he'd spent many a childhood lunchtime at Alma's table, eating alphabet soup and saltines. He looked helplessly at Karen.

"Can we do something for you?" Karen asked Tracey.

"There are things I wanted to put right," Tracey murmured. "I'm in a program." James feared she might cry, and he didn't think he could bear one more person's tears, not today. Karen had cried into the night but wouldn't allow James in the bed. He'd lain on the rug, using his overnight bag as a pillow. Karen had taken all the luggage when she left—a statement, he realized now, about his own physical and emotional absences—and he'd made do with the one bag ever since as a sort of penance.

Tracey glanced upstairs. "He doesn't seem to be coming back down."

The front door opened, and another small knot of people scattered through: aunts and cousins, more neighbors, some of Marie's coworkers from the library. Karen whispered to James: "See if you can get your father to come down here."

James watched his almost-ex-wife take Tracey into the kitchen. Then he turned, alone, to face the flight of stairs.

At his father's bedroom door his mother's dog, a grief-stricken Yorkie, sat like a broken doorstop, half-standing, half-sitting, its pindrop black eyes darting. James pushed the door open and found his father standing at the window, gazing down at the ark. The bed looked freshly made. "People are here, Dad," James said.

His father didn't move. He was wearing the suit he'd bought for James's graduation from Berkeley, over twenty years past; it fit him badly, and he looked like what he was: a pipefitter in a suit he'd been forced to put on. Because of the long, bitter mill strike, he hadn't worked in months, his retirement package suspended in a limbo he never talked about. James wondered if he should offer his father money.

"Dad, there are people downstairs." Without his mother here, he felt his sentences as ungainly blows, awkward as two-by-fours.

His father seemed blurred and ghostly in the cottony light blanketing through the window. Snow was coming. *Your father,* people had whispered to him all morning, *Your father, your poor father, he's been building that, that thing, whatever it is, and the mill's still out, and now that your mother's gone . . .* In his youth, James had sometimes felt orphaned by his parents' mutual devotion, but he felt nothing but pity now. Then, as his father turned to face him, another sensation altogether: a stab of envy, shockingly familiar. As he had once envied his father the breadth of his love, James now envied him the breadth of his grief. James himself would never suffer like this; he knew it; and the knowledge of what he'd been spared provided not a scrap of relief.

"Your mother had a lot of friends," his father said.

"It's you they're here to see, Dad. People come to, I don't know, to comfort the survivors."

His father turned to the window again. "I'd just as soon stay up here," he said. He took off the suit jacket. He sat down and removed his shoes, then lay across the made bed, eyes open and fixed on the ceiling. "I'd just as soon."

The dog slunk in and whined at the bedside. James stooped to pick it up. It was coarse and wiry and not at all the comfort he might have been hoping for. "You want the dog?" he asked.

His father nodded, and James placed the dog on the bed next to him. His father didn't move.

"Karen and I are getting a divorce, Dad."

His father blinked once, slowly. "Your mother figured it was something like that. She used to hear from Karen so regular."

"I'm sorry, Dad."

"It was good of her to come. Your mother would've wanted her here."

"I'm going downstairs now. People are here."

"All right." He put his big hand on the little dog.

"That's a nice-looking rig out there, Dad," James said. "Like a sculpture, kind of."

"I wanted to paint it. Your mother liked it better plain."

James waited. "All right, then. I'm going now."

Downstairs the rooms swelled with the murmurings of people who had known his mother far better than he. Most of the women brisked in and out of the kitchen; the men circulated uncomfortably, parting the drapes from time to time as if hoping for help. Brad Collins sat in Marie's chair, looking forlornly down at her knitting.

"He won't come down," James said to him. He had trailed Brad Collins for an entire summer more than thirty years ago, falling in with Brad's other kids and pretending he was Brad's son.

"Leave him alone, then," Brad said. He put his hand on James's arm, and for the first time since he'd gotten the news, James teared up.

"The dog is with him. I left the dog up there."

"Good. That's good." Brad nodded, his lower lip jutting out. "It was a great love story, James. Children don't know these things about their parents. Ernie and Marie. It was a great love story."

"I did know that," James assured him, nodding. "I knew that."

The afternoon unfolded, long and painful. Karen produced a coffee urn from someplace—where?—and it burbled efficiently. Finally the guests trickled out, even Brad and Alma, leaving James and Karen alone.

Then Tracey emerged from the kitchen. "Oh," James said.

"I didn't know anybody," she explained. "I guess I was hiding." Her coat was still on, the top button nearly twisted off.

James stood up: her cue to leave. He wanted to sit in his mother's chair and imagine what it might be like to love a woman the way his father had loved her.

"I hurt your mother," Tracey said, picking up her purse. "It's been a weight on my conscience. I mean, for years, like a big green fist, a monster's fist bearing down on my terrible conscience." She extracted a starched stack of bills. "I realize that money is a poor. . . I mean, some people might even consider this kind of crass, but an apology is not something you can hold in your hand, the only thing you can really hold in your hand is money, so this is heartfelt, I do assure you, and I'd appreciate your forebearance very, very much. I've been saving up. It's four hundred dollars."

"Please, keep your money," James said, shocked. "Whatever it is, I'm sure my mother's forgotten it." He didn't want to hear some story about hurt feelings, a women's squabble. Maybe she'd stolen some books from the library under his mother's watch. James looked past her, toward the stairs, where his father was descending in his new, vague way. He was still wearing most of the suit, the shirt damp and rumpled, the tie, too short, pasted askew on his broad chest. How long had he been like this, moving like a hurt deer? Is this what grief looked like?

Ernie faltered toward Marie's chair and stood there, kneading the chair-back hard with his meaty fingers. He fixed on Tracey. "What did you say your name was?"

"Tracey Martin," she said, blinking fast. "Used to be Brighton." She sucked up her breath as if expecting a blow.

After a long silence, in which something wrong and new racketed into the room, some knowledge James was not privy to but sensed in the shifting planes of his father's face, Ernie said: "There was a Tracey Brighton, a long time ago, broke into our cabin."

"That was me," Tracey said, her eyes brimming. "I was nineteen, Mr. Whitten, I'm a different person now."

James looked to Karen, who shook her head: *No, I have no idea.*

"I was a horrible person then, Mr. Whitten," Tracey was saying, "truly I was, I know that, but I swear to you I'm different now. I'm in a program, and a church, and I'm going to marry a wonderful man soon, a minister, but first there are certain steps, a certain clearing of conscience, and it was my idea completely, I assure you, nobody's making me do this, it's my own free will, I've become a person of free will"—she held out the money on her narrow palm—"and I sincerely wish to offer amends."

"You're talking about Bear Lake?" his father said, the planes in his face breaking up now, but subtly, like an earthquake too small to register. "You and that boyfriend of yours? Our place on Bear Lake?"

James looked around, bewildered. His father and this stranger were discussing the family camp, sold the year after James left for Berkeley.

His father's face continued to transform itself, an expression James remembered from the few times, as a mouthy teenager, he'd suffered Ernie's rage. Always it was about defending Marie, defending his wife against the rudeness of his son. "They gave you a wrist-slap," his father was saying, his voice shimmering with fury. "You came into the courtroom with your lawyer father and your pretty dress and got a wrist-slap."

"What's going on?" James asked, his blood beginning to pulse woozily. "Dad, what are you talking about?"

Tracey began to weep, her palm still open, money stacked like a deck of cards. Karen shot James a look: *Do something.*

"When I got there she was bleeding," his father said. "Her little hands were tied, and her ankles." He looked at James, a scary, loosened look. "Your mother was a husky woman, a strong woman. But she had such little hands." Before James could stop him, he lunged at Tracey. "You get out of my wife's house!" he raged, his face finally crumpling like burnt steel. Both fists bunched and shook. "Get out, get out of her house!"

Tracey flinched violently, then bolted for the front door, flinging the words *I'm sorry I'm sorry I'm sorry* like coins over her shoulder. When the door shuddered closed, the house fell silent.

"For God's sake," James said, trembling now. "Dad?" He approached his father as he would an accident victim, with all due fear and attention. Ernie was still standing, his fists at his ears, tears dripping helplessly down his windburned cheeks.

"Your mother loved that place," he said heavily. "We sold it because of that tramp and her burglar boyfriend."

"A burglary?" James asked, unable to focus, turning from Karen, whose eyes looked pinned open, to his father, who kept shaking his head, looking down upon Marie's chair. "Why didn't I know about this?" James pleaded, his head vibrating like a stuck saw.

"The boyfriend got some jail time," Ernie said, taking long, wet breaths. "They broke in, and took some things, and the car. First they cut your mother with a knife," he said. "The girl's the one who did it. A little cut"—he touched his own face, just above the temple, his hand quivering—"right here. Just to scare her. Just to make her think there was no such a thing as being safe in the world." He bent his head, all the light in the room seeming to pool in on him.

"Good God," Karen breathed, dropping into a chair.

James squinted hard, trying vainly to clear his view. "When, Dad? When did this happen?"

"You'd just gone off to Berkeley. Your mother wanted to be alone, so she went up to the camp."

"Alone?" James asked. His mother never went to camp alone. His mother never went anywhere alone.

Ernie shook his head, then made his way into Marie's chair. He picked up a skein of yarn and held it. "She was under the boyfriend's spell," he muttered. "That's what she said in court. Your mother believed her. Her in her pretty dress. All that blond hair." He clutched the yarn.

"Of all days," he said. "Your mother would think it had some kind of, some kind of significance. That it meant I was supposed to forgive her."

He looked at James, as if James would not know this about his mother. Ernie waved his hands, washing them of the whole tottering world. "Of all days. Why today, of all days?" He dropped his head into his hands, rocking himself a little.

"What was Mom doing there by herself?" James asked. He was trying to backtrack, get one fact at a time. He would build himself back to steady ground this way.

"We had some trouble," his father said at last. "Your mother and I, we hit a bump in the road."

All right, James thought. Fact number one. "So she, what, moved up there?" He couldn't imagine it. "She moved up to camp?"

His father looked up. "It was a big bump."

Now James sat, his skin throbbing, the house groaning with his mother's absence. It was his own self unbuckling now, everything he thought he knew sluicing away. The endlessly told story of his parents' smooth slide into love, that beautiful, seamless ride against which he had measured his own failures of affection—that story suddenly read more like anybody else's, maybe even his own if you didn't count the ending.

"Are you all right, Ernie?" Karen asked.

James watched, stranded by confusion, as Karen shepherded Ernie into the kitchen. He heard the tap opening, a chair scraping back, a low, encouraging murmur.

He stepped outside, taking in painful gulps of air, imagining the hundred other ways his marriage might have gone. It had started to snow, a lacy feathering that landed wet and silent. He was about to retreat when he spotted Tracey, parked across the street, waiting. He marched over to her as she rolled down her window. "Get out," he told her.

"You take this money," she snapped, thrusting the bills into his hands. "I won't leave till you take it. I mean it."

He saw just then a snippet of the hardness she'd been trying to overcome. It pleased him unaccountably, the aftermath of a bad life still present in her voice. He reached into the car and slapped the bills down on the dashboard. "You cut my mother's face."

She nodded gravely. Her upturned face looked puffy and stained. "He told me to do worse than that. I saved your mother's neck, is what really happened."

"And you want, what, a medal for that?"

"I never wanted to hurt her. You have to believe me, I had nightmares for years."

"You—" It hurt to talk, as if his throat had been badly bruised and only halfway healed. He managed to say, "What are you looking for? Forgiveness?"

She shook her head, her mouth melting downward. "No," she said. "But I was hoping."

Snow filtered down the back of his shirt. He stepped back, eyeing her corded neck, her old eyes, her shabby car. "Just go. Keep your guilt money."

"Wait," she said. "Please. I have to tell you something. Your mother wasn't scared of me. I was a desperate little loser with a knife, but she wasn't scared." She blinked at the snow falling into her open window. "I think it was because she could see I was redeemable."

James stood in the spongy street, gazing at this luck-less, hapless, used-up person who had come up from Connecticut with a stack of new bills. What on earth would his mother have done?

"I've got two kids now," she said. "Two ex-husbands." She made a laugh-cry sound and wiped her eyes again. "You want to talk baggage, I've got a trainload, and yet as soon as I'm finished paying my moral debts, this wonderful guy is going to marry me. He pulled me out of the muck and still he's going to marry me."

James glanced up the street, and down. His mother would have stood here, listening. This was a son's knowledge and he was glad to have it. He leaned on the car door. "How many," he asked, "how many debts do you have to repay?"

"More than I can do," she said. "They're hard to track down. I found your parents from the court record."

"Are they all like this?"

She shrugged. "One guy slapped me, but at least he took the money. Listen, do you want to get in? You're all wet."

He studied her for a few moments, then rounded the car and got in beside her. Vinyl seats, no floor mats, a wicker cross dangling from the rearview. He felt a pang of pity that he hoped his mother would approve of. "Everybody has debts," he said.

"Well, my conscience is in worse shape than most people's."

It occurred to James then, sitting in this car that smelled faintly of transmission fluid, that Tracey's conscience was probably in better shape than most people's.

Better than his, certainly. The car's bare interior seemed muffled and safe. He envied her the luxury of confession. To whom could he confess?

I never loved my wife. I carried on with women half my age. I was a terrible father. I was a terrible son.

"There's no such thing as a clean conscience," he told her. "You won't feel as cleansed as you think you will." Tracey regarded him without pity, without judgment; it was the way he imagined alcoholics met one another at AA meetings. "It's never too late to start fresh," she offered.

"Oh, it is," he said. "It is absolutely too late." He looked out through the scrim of snow at his parents' house. "Some things aren't amendable."

"That's true," she agreed. "But some things are." She held his gaze. "I was hoping this would be one of them."

The world seemed so full of transgressions at the moment, so full there was hardly room to take a breath. To erase just one, to have that power, did not seem like something he could turn down. He felt useful. He felt called. "Listen," he told her. "I'm her son. I can forgive you on her behalf."

"Really?" she said, her lips parting. "Oh. Wow. My God. Thank you, really. You have no idea."

She slipped the money from the dashboard and he took it. She shuddered with relief. If his father refused the money, he would send it to his daughter in Alaska, or wherever she was by the time they got back. Karen would know; Karen would know precisely.

He shut the door and headed across the street, hunching his shoulders against the snow. Behind him he could hear Tracey's car rattle into gear. Ahead of him lay his father's house, and the ark, steadfast and hulking, seemed to move as the snow gathered upon it. He stood staring at it despite the cold, this object of mystery that belonged to one man and one woman upon whom some trouble had been visited, failing to put them asunder.

He entered the house, which had gone silent. Karen was sitting in his mother's chair. "He's upstairs," she said. She shook her head slowly. "God, Jamie."

"I know. God."

"People have all kinds of secrets," she said. She gazed up at him. "Did you think I'd come back? After you were finished with Miss Teenage America?"

He tilted his head to really see her; she was not angry. "I think so," he admitted. "Probably."

"There was a time when I might have," she said. "But not now. You know that, right?"

He nodded. "I'm so sorry," he told her, enunciating the words.

She smiled wearily. "Thanks."

"Can I sit with you awhile?" he asked.

She slid over. His mother's chair wasn't big enough for the two of them, but he wedged himself next to her, sliding his arm along her shoulders. The coming evening edged in, certain and safe, as reassuring as the long-ago feel of his mother's hand. He listened for sounds of his father. After a few minutes his hip fell asleep, his knee began to throb. But he didn't move. Something about the waning of this sorrowful day felt wondrous and unearned, like a snow day or a magic spell or forgiveness, and James did not want to be the one to end it.

Take Care Good Boy

KENNY LOVE, *student and searcher*

Kenny Love sauntered home from his shift at the VideoMart to find the kitchen lights on and his father and stepmother looking at him as if he'd just walked off a spaceship. His father announced, "Your mother's uncle died." This would be Uncle Ellery, his mother's only relative.

Before Kenny could decide how he felt about his great-uncle's passing, his father handed him a letter—a dry boilerplate explaining that Ellery Lydon had bequeathed to Kenny Love his house in Long Ridge, all its contents, and nine thousand dollars *to do with as he wished*. He could take possession, if he so desired, on the seventh of February. The remainder of the estate was going to an outfit called Feathered Friends.

Kenny stared at the letter. He had met his great-uncle only once, when he was eight, just before his mother left. They lived in Connecticut then: he remembered a long car ride to Maine, his mother steering with one hand and with the other punching the buttons on the radio.

"Is this a joke?" he asked. His father could not be trusted even in minor matters.

"What it is, Kenny, is an opportunity," said his father, a hawk-nosed ectomorph who liked to display his long, artistic fingers by draping them over chair arms. "You can sell the place and put the money toward your tuition."

"I'm keeping it," Kenny said, deciding on the spot. "I'm moving there."

His father went on as if he hadn't heard. "You'll work at that video joint till next fall, just as we planned, and then honor your commitment to Harvard University." The way his father always added "University" to "Harvard" made Kenny, a devout pacifist, want to rip his father's lungs out through his throat.

"I don't have a commitment."

His father's eyes went steely. "If you think I'm going to let you sidewind your career at Harvard University just because of this goddamned Thoreau kick—"

"It's not a kick," Kenny said. "I told you fifty times I wasn't going."

Now Cindy chimed in: "Why didn't Faye's uncle leave the place to Faye?"

"He left the bulk to a bunch of birds, all right?" his father said. "Old bachelors go funny at the end."

His father's words hurt. Kenny lifted his fist, in which the letter crackled agreeably. "Wasn't this addressed to me?" he asked, tight-lipped.

"It was from an attorney-at-law, Kenny," Cindy said. "Your father had to open it." She said "attorney-at-law" as if she were reading him a scary story.

"Thoreau went to Harvard," his father said.

Kenny narrowed his eyes. "He refused to accept his diploma."

After a long, melodramatic argument in which Kenny held fast, his plan forming beautifully in his head, his father concluded feebly: "You've got a mind for math, Kenny, not philosophy. This is a stupid, kid stunt." His mouth continued to move, but he was psychologically hog-tied and he knew it.

Kenny felt hot with power, giddy with it. He was no kid; he was a seventeen-year-old man about to graduate from high school an entire semester early, working thirty hours a week for road money. In truth he hadn't expected to save enough for the sort of wilderness experience he had in mind. He'd thought of trekking through Alaska, exploring the Amazon, camping on the banks of Lake Victoria, some form of extended meditation that would require a Thoreauvian purity of body and soul that he did not expect to encounter at a dorm party. Now, amazingly, God and his great-uncle had dropped a ready-made meditation into his lap at the eleventh hour. He saluted his father and Cindy, then spun out the door.

Throughout that long, cold, meaningful evening, Kenny sat on a bluff overlooking the smelly Maine town his father had settled him in. Kenny hated this town, which had the nerve to call itself a city. For going on a year now, the place had been tense and coiled and strike-ravaged. His small group of friends, normally placid and aimless, had divided into passionately separate camps—scab sons against striker sons—leaving Kenny, the sole professor's son, floating out on the fringes, irrelevant, which is how he'd felt in every place he'd ever lived.

It was Thoreau who had saved him, who had painted a romantic halo around the razored edges of his aloneness. He would make his cash bonus last two years, the same amount of time Thoreau had taken to find his soul. He would live in Ellery Lydon's house—he remembered it as a simple cabin surrounded by firs—freed from the small-minded politics of so-called civilized life, freed from the caprice of so-called friendships. He would ponder his place in the universe, something his father seemed utterly incapable of despite those drapey fingers.

In the end it was Cindy who drove him northward to his inherited house. She took a day off from her flower shop and added a basket of red carnations to the few things Kenny had packed into the trunk. From day one Cindy had been bribing Kenny and Francine with good deeds and floral arrangements. Francine had fallen hard; their mother had been gone for many years and Francine, who was thirteen and fat, didn't appear fussy about who might take her place. "You don't have the constitution for this, Kenny," Francine said, hopping into the front seat. Apparently Cindy had invited her along. "Wilderness experiences test your grit."

"Talk like a normal person, Francine," Kenny told her.

Francine folded her arms, haughty as a schoolmarm. "I'm just *saying*, you weren't raised gritty."

Cindy started the car. "Experience increases our wisdom but doesn't reduce our follies," she said, quoting, as was her wont, from her daily planner. At the last possible second, Kenny's father strode stone-faced to the car and they shook hands through the window—a mulish formality, since they had not spoken a civil word for weeks.

The ride to Ellery Lydon's house took three hours. A light, dry snow fell briefly, the Christmasy kind that made Kenny feel like a character in a movie, a man on his way to boot camp or a gold rush, leaving the womenfolk behind. The house, a well-appointed bungalow with black wooden shutters, sat at the end of a bleak, sparsely inhabited outskirt road. Empty fields fell away from both sides of the house, and the lot resembled one of those grief-stricken landscapes from a Wyeth painting. Away down the back field, the terrain rose sharply to a four-mile crew cut of firs that gave Long Ridge its name.

"This looks cozy," Cindy said, pulling over. Though the house was missing the tight circle of trees Kenny had added to his memory, the inside was almost exactly as he remembered it: spare, pleasant rooms scented with pipe tobacco. His father's house, with Cindy's frothy touches, seemed silly and irrelevant by contrast. As Cindy and Francine helped bring in his things, he tried to remember more of his visit here: a smallish man with enormous hands; birds ribboning around the yard; ginger ice cream. His mother, tall and jittery, smoking a cigarette, staring out the kitchen door at the broad back field.

"Some wilderness," Francine said from the parlor. "The phone works."

"It's a rotary," Cindy said. "Isn't that precious?"

Indeed, everything worked. Nothing had been turned off or shut down, as if Ellery had been loath to let an inconvenience like his own death mar the running of his household. Kenny offered Cindy and Francine a drink of water from the kitchen tap—*his* kitchen tap. The water ran cold and clear. "Kenny," Francine said, gaping at him, mournful as a puppy. "Why didn't he leave me anything?"

"Probably he didn't know about you," Kenny said. "Mom's not big on updates."

"Oh, Kenny," Cindy said, "I'm sure that's not true." She rested her hand on Francine's shoulder. "Your great-uncle probably thought you were too young for an inheritance, honey."

But Kenny knew better. Their mother had dumped the two of them with no ceremony—no tears or parting words that Kenny could recall—to move to London, England, in the hope of taking up a new life. She called the two of them once a year on her birthday, a thread of contact between their brief summer visits to her depressing apartment in the theater district, where she edited copy for a science magazine.

Suddenly Kenny felt sentimental, remembering how Francine had followed him like an imprinted gosling in the months and years after their mother left. Evenings, their father out somewhere and the rented house quiet, Francine liked to pull up her own chair next to Kenny's bedroom desk as he labored over vocabulary words and long division, or, later, algebra or chemistry or world history, her cheek resting on one plump hand, her watchful eyes tracing the jottings of his pencil. He always let her stay there, understanding even as a younger boy that his sister felt safe in the warm circle of light from his desk lamp, that the sound of his pencil felt pacifying, a steady presence. From time to time he would look up from his homework and encounter his sister's face, as sweet and round as an apple; she waited for him to smile at her, and he did. She didn't ask for or seem to require anything more than his knowledge that she existed. In the three years since Cindy's arrival, Francine had stopped trailing her brother, in fact had started second-guessing his opinions, bestowing unwanted advice, reading his favorite books for an alternate interpretation; but he liked to think of his sister's impudence as another form of worship.

He was just beginning to imagine a tender good-bye wherein he parted the flat planes of his baby sister's hair, the better to see tears silvering beneath her sad, oversized glasses—but Francine's mood had changed utterly. "You're a coward for leaving us," she told him in a soft, quavering voice, and then she called him a rotten lousy yellowbelly in a voice that could start a tractor, and then, having stomped down the front steps toward the car, she turned in her tracks to inform him in another voice altogether—an eerie, otherworldly voice as creepy as a sleeping snake—that Henry David Thoreau's sister had come for her brother's laundry twice a month and that his mother brought him meals.

"That's not true," Kenny said, shocked. But it probably was. Even angry, Francine never lied.

"Look it up, Brother," she snapped, and that word, *Brother*, left him feeling slapped and stunned.

"She'll get over it," Cindy assured him, and it occurred to him then that he'd been stolen from, that Cindy had taken the one thing he'd always been able to count on. She left the carnations on a chair and flurried after Francine. "Francine," Kenny called after her. "Francine, come on." From behind her closed window Cindy shook her head at him, helpless. The car ground into gear and they were gone.

Kenny stood on his doorstep in the cold, listening to the car engine fade into the white silence of road. This was solitude. It was he who had gone. The burden of his family seemed to lift like the smallest wings at his back.

He walked out to the road, turned around, then re-entered his new house, alone. He spent the afternoon tracking over the bowed floors, dragging his fingers over his great-uncle's dusty things. Certain items amongst the clutter struck him as richly weighted: a pipe cocked into the steel dimple of an ashtray stand; cat dishes stacked into the dish drainer; a pair of gum boots set a stance apart as if intending to walk off by themselves. The stairs to the second floor were steep and bare, the one bedroom a perfect square with a single bed in an iron frame and a bedstand spilling over with the reading matter of a man who loved the world.

Around suppertime he walked a scant ten minutes to the town of Long Ridge—a flattened break in the landscape with one intersection, a diner, a grocery store, and, he was vaguely humiliated to note, a laundromat. He bought some groceries at the Pick-and-Pay with the first fifty dollars of his nine thousand. He carried his groceries in a backpack down the flat, woods-scented road, waving mightily to a neighbor, who responded with a puzzled bob of the head. Though it was a far cry from a trek through

Thoreau's woods, to Kenny, who had been dragged by the hand from one town to another since he was old enough to walk, a trip to the grocery was the equivalent of killing and eating a bear.

When he approached the house again, seeing its odd, ladylike shutters and surrounding fields, he felt changed. Trusted. Or, more precisely, entrusted *to*. He found a bag of bird seed in the shed and filled Ellery's barren feeders, and before long the four corners of the house thronged with tiny, garrulous birds. When the time came he took his place at Ellery's kitchen table, set down his steaming plastic tray of Stouffer's chicken with mushroom sauce, cracked open a ginger ale, and nearly wept with happiness.

His plan was to write a memoir, to surprise himself with what he might glean from nature's relentless rhythms. His secret hope was for young men generations hence to seek the contemplations of Kenny Love for inspiration and re-assurance, the way he turned to Thoreau. His lofty goal embarrassed him a little (he imagined the title: *Essays of a Man*) but not enough to be turned from the task. He rummaged through his duffel for his brand-new journal, a hardbound tablet with gauzy pages meant for his new fountain pen. He fit some wood into the parlor stove, set-tled into Ellery's wingbacked chair, and placed his feet on Ellery's strange, tasseled hassock. Once, twice, he tried lighting Ellery's pipe, then abandoned it to the ashtray stand. On the first page of his journal he wrote, *February 7: Kenny's life begins.*

The mantel clock ticked portentously, but what it portended Kenny could not imagine. The quiet felt like a dead man's wish; it unnerved him, rattled his confidence. The page before him seemed to whiten as he ruminated on the fact that he'd never loved a girl, that he claimed no true friends, that the town he'd left was inflamed by passions he had no access to, and that the night drifting down on his great-uncle's home was vast and grave and moonless. He picked up the phone and dialed Francine, who was always good for an argument, but she refused to speak to him and he had to listen instead to Cindy's fulminations on the special sensitivities of thirteen-year-old girls.

The night persisted, thick as lint behind the plain blue curtains. Ellery had no TV, and Kenny had left behind, in his old life, his computer, his stereo, even his calculator. The predictions of calculus would do him no good here. He went upstairs to unpack his clothes, hanging his shirts among Ellery's in the cedar closet. Here he found the calendars.

There were over fifty of them, calendars of the sort meant to hang on kitchen doors. From the wild variety in theme—Tripp's Farm and Feed 1948, Tropical Flowers 1963, Kliban Cats 1978—Kenny discerned that his great-uncle had made his annual selections solely for the amount of white space in the daily squares, which were crowded with notations in robust handwriting that became weak and spidery over the years. Ellery had come back from the Second World War with a bum leg and a passion for all things living, despite losing a sweetheart to his high school rival. These facts Kenny gleaned by

·

sifting through the earliest calendars, in which Ellery recorded visits from friends, the exertions of his many cats, the inching progress of the yard and garden, and almost nothing of his work as a plumber. In time, people dropped out of the entries one by one, and the calendars became less a journal than a collection of field notes about birds and woodchucks and weather and the ever-present cats. In July 1978 Ellery had required five squares to describe a robin stabbing a caterpillar to death under the rose trellis.

This was more than Kenny could have hoped for: his great-uncle had been a modern-day Thoreau. There wasn't much in the way of embellishment, but then his great-uncle's gift was for observation; Kenny himself would supply the philosophy. He would begin tomorrow, February 8: armed with notations from more than fifty February eighths, Kenny would walk his uncle's winter fields in search of the mackerel sky from 1956, the lone robin from 1967, the collapsed fox den from 1981. In his current state of spiritual blindness, approaching the world with another man's eyes seemed an idea blessed by God.

He returned to the pipe-scented hold of his great-uncle's chair and spent the night's quietest hours there, searching. Long after midnight he found a notation for July 11, 1990: *Faye stopped by with her boy a good boy.* Instantly Kenny remembered Marmalade, the heavy orange cat that had crept down from the jam closet to fill up his great-uncle's arms. He remembered a big, unexpected, booming laugh, and his mother's awful pacing. Except for that one maddeningly brief notation, he found no other reference to his mother or himself, nothing to account for his inheritance.

A good boy. Ellery Lydon had seen something in little Kenny Love all the way back when he was eight. Something—and what could it be?—that impelled him to leave his home to a boy he barely knew. He looked around at Ellery's things in the quiet of the waning night. He put on the woolen overalls hanging by the back door. He tried the gum boots and walked up the stairs and down. He read twenty pages of one of the books on Ellery's nightstand, *Birds and Their Ways.* Then he made up his great-uncle's bed and slept fitfully, waking for good at dawn.

It had snowed overnight, an airy shawl of the bitterest white covering Ellery's morning fields. Kenny shoveled the walk, urging his back and shoulders into every heft. On February 8, 1965, Ellery had done this very thing, probably with this same shovel. After he finished, Kenny gathered up some calendars and walked in his great-uncle's boots to the Long Ridge Diner, troubled by a mysterious longing and wishing he could remember what he'd done to be marked down as a good boy.

The diner was warm and bright, filled with the sound of cheap crockery and human voices. He smiled up at the waitress, a fading, middle-aged redhead whose uniform fit her like a sausage casing. "What'll it be, kiddo?" she asked him, balancing a coffeepot in one hand, the other hand fisted against an impressive shelf of hip.

"Name's Ellery," Kenny said abruptly. "Ellery Lydon." Then he noticed her name tag. "Your name Iris?"

"Actually, it's Lady of Spain. I just wear this tag for

yucks." She set the coffeepot down. "Any relation to the Ellery Lydon on the ridge road?"

He turned his cup over and she poured. "My uncle. My mother's uncle, actually. We were really tight." He tapped the calendars at his elbow. "I think you're in here."

He opened the final calendar, which he'd removed from the door going down to the cellar. He showed her the weakly rendered, cryptic messages: November 1: *Deer in north field.* November 2: *Iris brought soup very tasty.* November 3: *Stayed in bed cats not happy.* Then, on November 4, the last entry, like dying words: *Take care.*

"He died on the tenth," Iris said, puddling up. "I checked on him after he'd missed too many breakfasts. I took him to the hospital, and that was that." Iris had a sweet, unlined face and wide gray eyes; Kenny wondered if his great-uncle might have been a little in love with her. She turned the calendar back a month and traced her finger over Ellery's last weeks, a chronicle, as in years past, of the change of season: the death rattle of a few undropped leaves, the hailing cry of red-tails overhead. On October 31 he'd written: *Ermine in the woodpile today happy halloween.*

"What's an ermine?" Kenny asked Iris.

"A weasel, basically. They turn white in winter. You want some breakfast?"

Kenny nodded, deciding not to admit he thought an ermine was a type of ladies' coat. He tried to divine a philosophical context for an ermine in a woodpile. Beauty? Survival? But he knew nothing of ermines: perhaps they were ugly creatures, near extinction.

When Iris came back with a stack of pancakes, she studied him for a moment or two. "If Ellery was your mother's uncle, how come your name's Lydon and not something else?"

"My father took my mother's name," Kenny said, blinking slowly, amazed at his sudden capacity to lie on the fly.

"He did?"

"He's a sculptor."

"No kidding. We got a few artists living up here. What kind of art does he sculpt?"

"Crap, mostly. He welds these gigantic Tinkertoys out of sheet metal just so he can show off for the college girls."

She looked interested. "Do they fall for it?"

"My stepmother did. She's no girl, though. She just acts like one."

"You should show more respect, Ellery," she said. "How old are you? Fifteen?"

"Twenty-one."

She laughed. "If you're twenty-one, I'm a supermodel." She pulled a set of keys out of her apron pocket. "These are yours, I guess. Ellery asked me to keep an eye on the place till somebody showed up. He was typically tight-lipped about who. You owe me for December's bills. January's haven't come in yet."

"How much?" Kenny asked, alarmed.

Iris shrugged. "Not much. Ellery was frugal as all get-out. Course, you would know that, being his namesake and all." She looked him over. "Anyway, he was a nice man. We used to go bird-watching together."

Kenny glanced outside as if a bird might be winging by, but all he could see was the neon beer sign in the window of the Pick-and-Pay. Francine had been right, it was no wilderness; but it would do. To partake of the world's worst temptations—superstores, restaurants and bars, twelve-screen multiplexes—Kenny would have to drive a very long distance, and of course he didn't have a car.

"Thanks for looking in on my place. I figured it was the lawyer."

Iris thought this was hilarious, and laughed until Kenny wished she'd stop. "Oh," she said. "Oh, aren't you the funniest thing." She put her hands on her hips. "You know, I think you might look like him a little."

"My mother said that once."

After that Kenny ate in silence, sifting through the calendars. The morning's snowfall had brought him nothing beyond the simple facts of snow and shovel, facts already recorded in a calendar thirty years old. So far, the unadorned motions of his great-uncle's routines defied interpretation. When Iris came to clear his plate, he asked for another order of pancakes, not wanting to leave. She raised her eyebrows.

"Man's gotta eat, Iris," he said, words that sounded like something his father would say to this very waitress, hoping she might catch a whiff of double meaning, not that his father would have the slightest interest in a woman like Iris, but he would want her to want him, to think it fleetingly possible, then he would saunter out under the delicious fading heat of her eyes. That these words had come from his mouth sickened him, and he instantly told Iris his real name.

"Kenny Love?" she said. "Really?"

He nodded contritely. "I'd rather be named Ellery Lydon, to be honest. It was kind of hard to resist."

"Is that an apology?"

He nodded.

"Then I accept," she said, sitting down, her perfume a lilac that Kenny found shockingly attractive. He hoped what he felt at this moment—a deeply ambiguous longing for entirely the wrong person—did not descend from his father.

"Did you go to the funeral?" he asked.

"There wasn't any," she said. "He's buried up at St. Joe's." Her bright eyes shone down on him.

"I just met him once, actually," he admitted. "I was eight." He looked up. "What happened to the cats?"

"I took the young ones. The old ones I had put down."

"You the one who washed the dishes?"

She nodded.

"Do you know what a red-tail is?" he asked.

"It's a hawk."

"They're in here a lot," he said, his hand on the calendars.

"Ellery was a nature boy. You want to know what's in the air or under the ground, you ask Ellery." She smiled sadly. "Not that anybody did. He was kind of shy."

"I'm like that," Kenny said quietly.

"That's all right, Ellery," she said. "Extroverts are over-rated." He waited for her to bring the second round of pancakes, glad that he'd told her his real name and that she'd called him Ellery just the same. The pancakes were surprisingly good. The world, as it turned out, was full of surprises.

KENNY HAD not counted on the sprawling length of days spent alone. At the end of each day his most vivid recollection was chatting with Iris in the diner way back at breakfast time. "Every damn morning," Iris said after the second week. "I thought the point was solitude." He ate his morning pancakes despite her chiding, and only mortification prevented him from returning for lunch. He could not help wondering how Ellery had braced himself against the winter silence, the early dark, the absence of human voices. He read sections of *Walden* until he had them by heart, but felt each day as a kind of loss. His job at the VideoMart had been simple, mindless in ways, but there was always someone to talk to. And though his father spent most of his time brooding, Francine was never short an opinion, and Cindy's foamy exclamations had a way of filling a place with sound.

The truth was, he missed talking. All he'd managed to add to Ellery's sightings were a few sightings of his own: on day twelve he'd spooked a flock of tiny, quarreling birds he couldn't name. When he tried to pry from their erupting flight a poetic line for his white, white journal, what popped into his head was the formula for instantaneous velocity. In his old life he might have spent some long, thick hours with a calculator, but here, where the theoretical predictions of calculus resided so far from the visible world, he could only look at these birds and envy them their voices.

Ellery's final calendars darkened with bad news: December 27, 1997: *Fred's funeral down to Rockland.* August 30, 1998: *Sadie Hoffman another one gone.*

Kenny read them through, thinking that Thoreau had had it easy, following no footsteps but his own. In his two long weeks of solitude Kenny had become convinced that the last, ardent message, *Take care*, had been written expressly to him. In his head Kenny ran Ellery's messages together: *Take care good boy.* In answer, he watched light change over the short course of a winter day; in answer, he walked the fields and roads in the cold; in answer, he read endlessly about solitude and still waters and the glory of a reddening sky.

On day nineteen, Kenny took Ellery's binoculars from a hook near the kitchen door and clomped out to gaze down the long back field the way he imagined Ellery had. He scanned the wood-pile for an ermine. He'd forgotten to ask Iris how big an ermine might be—he imagined a squirrel-sized animal, but realized with no small trepidation that an ermine might be groundhog-sized, maybe bigger. He checked the sky for hawks, then set out to patrol the fields for animal tracks till his toes went numb. He found path upon path of prints, some deep and cloven, some light and starlike, others no more than a breath of air on the snow. All these separate journeys, crossing back and forth over each other, begot in him a type of happiness that felt perilous, vaguely ill-gotten. *Take care good boy*. Yes, he wanted to. But his great-uncle's house was plumb and well-kept, with nothing so much as a loose window sash for a hungry young man to apply himself to. Ellery's sightings, transcribed almost verbatim into Kenny's journal whether Kenny had observed them or not, bore the alarming mark of completeness.

As he neared the house again, he saw what he thought might be a woodchuck, or perhaps an ermine after all, sitting on a bristly hillock in the east field. He lifted the binoculars. The creature—which was not a woodchuck, not at all—stilled his blood.

It was an owl. A big owl. A tremendous owl, with a thick helmet of a head, a face framed by a dark, delicate parentheses of feathers, and savage, mean-gleaming yellow eyes staring straight through him.

"Holy," Kenny whispered. "Holy, holy." He became aware of an almost otherworldly silence, then realized that the bird feeders had been abandoned utterly.

He eased into the house and the owl stayed where it was, composed and silent. Kenny grabbed a field guide, raked through the pages, and found it—a Great Gray Owl, which according to the book belonged at least a thousand miles from Ellery Lydon's east field. Kenny flipped through every February since 1945—nothing. He sprinted down to the diner.

"Have you ever seen a Great Gray Owl?" he asked Iris.

She laughed. "In my dreams."

"There's one in Ellery's field."

She paused a long time, while he listened to the clatter of spoons. "It's probably a Great Horned."

"It has yellow eyes."

She paused again, scanning the room, counting tables. "Look, I have to finish up here. You go back and keep an eye on it."

"Is this a big deal?"

"Not if it's a Great Horned. Now go."

He went home. The owl had moved from the east field into the back, and waited, immense and still, about thirty yards from the kitchen door. It seemed to watch him. The earth fell quiet, and the most dire loneliness Kenny had ever known fumed geyserlike in his chest. To his amazement he began to weep, not because he was lonely, but because he had always been lonely, and because there existed in the world legions of creatures and plants and cloud formations that he had never once noticed, or, worse, never even thought to look for. He had been far too busy consorting with temporary friends, listening to music with crummy lyrics, fumbling with any girl who would let him, resenting his father, memorizing formulas, and hating the entire country of England because his mother had chosen to live there. He had been sound asleep for seventeen years, and this errant creature seemed to know it, staring and staring with those yellow, yellow eyes.

Finally Iris arrived, swaddled in a blue pea coat with a pair of expensive-looking binoculars hanging from her neck. She looked skeptical, but Kenny could see the pink of expectation in her cheeks.

"Right there," Kenny said, leading her out back.

She lifted the binoculars. "Jesus, Mary, and Joseph,"

she said. "Oh, I don't *believe* Ellery's missing this." She turned to him, her smooth cheeks spotted with cold. "Listen to me," she said, sounding like an emergency worker at an earthquake. "I'm going to put the word out. You'll have the local bird nuts here within the hour. After that it'll be Grand Central for days, birders from as far south as Philadelphia."

"You're kidding, right?" Kenny asked.

Iris shook her head. "They had a Boreal owl in Damariscotta about ten years ago and had to put a cop on traffic detail."

"Whoa."

She laughed again. "Oh, Ellery must be so *mad*." She laid her hands on Kenny's arms. "Listen to me, Ellery. You'll just have to enjoy it for him. Lap it up."

He stood alone for the next fifteen minutes watching the owl in the cold. At one point it raised its ponderous wings and lifted from the earth, drifting down a few feet to the west. "Stay, stay," he whispered, wholly believing he'd been summoned to this place by a dead man to witness a marvel in his stead. He remembered being shown this very field, white with potato blossoms, on that long-ago visit. Looking at the owl, he felt something closing behind him, profound and irreversible. He went back into Ellery's house and called London.

"You're *living* there?" his mother said. "You moved *in*?"

"Do you remember when we visited here? I was eight."

"Weren't you scheduled to start classes this term?" The way she said "classes" annoyed him. His mother had been placing "ah"s in words like *class* since she'd landed on English soil to buy a new life with her alimony checks.

"Mom. The visit. Do you remember it?"

"What is your father saying about all this? Why didn't he call me? That man never tells me anything."

"Mom, listen. When we visited Ellery."

She sighed. "Kenny, I don't know. I don't remember. What are you doing for money?"

"Mom."

Another sigh. "What."

"Aren't you sad, even a little, that he died?"

"Well, of course I'm sad. He was a nice man."

His mother floated at the other end of the line for a few seconds, an ocean away. He could barely conjure an image of her face. He tried to imagine the young wife about to leave her sculptor, bringing the boy to see her uncle. The good boy.

Then he knew.

"You asked him for money," Kenny said.

"Who?"

"Ellery. When you brought me here. You came for money so you could move to goddamned England."

He heard her light a cigarette. "Your father was screwing college girls, Kenny," she said. "Somehow this is all my fault?"

"Was he supposed to see how mature I was? How well I could handle being left?" When she didn't respond, he added, "You didn't tell him about Francine, did you? He never even knew you had another kid."

"This is none of your business, Kenny."

"Well, Francine did fine," he said, hoping to hurt her. "You should see how she's glommed onto Cindy." He waited a moment to calm down, and the owl helped, that imperious presence in the back field. Finally he asked his mother, "Were you close? You and your uncle?"

His mother laughed her sad London laugh. "Oh, Kenny. Nobody in my family was close."

When he hung up he glanced around Ellery's kitchen, at his herb pots on the windowsills, all his simple goods. Now Kenny saw this place as an apology. Money had changed hands, his mother had fled, and Ellery was the kind of man who would have felt sorry for the good boy left behind. And if he'd known about the good girl, the four-year-old girl his mother hadn't mentioned? Something twisted inside him, a physical hurt which he took for the spiritual waking he had so wished for. If this place was an apology, then Francine deserved it, too.

Outside, two cars pulled up, expelling big-eyed people in bright parkas carrying all manner of optics, looking up, around, then starting uncertainly down his vacant drive. Iris pulled up behind them and leaped out, directing the little band like a tour guide. They were chatty and animated, like the birds, ambassadors of the teeming world. He opened the door and waved, shrugging on his great-uncle's field coat. In his head he was already interviewing deserving buyers, gentling the house into another man's care, splitting the proceeds with Francine. He would keep the pipe and the ashtray stand and the soft winged chair. He would twine the calendars and his own pallid notebook into a keepsake bound with ribbon or string. He would return to the enraged town where he did not fit in, and leave again when it was time.

The bird-watchers had gathered out back. One of them squealed with discovery, her mitten lifting like a flag. Kenny opened a tin of coffee, stacked ten cups—all he had—on the table, took some muffins from the freezer. Time felt short and tottering. He pulled on Ellery's boots and went out to greet them, then showed them the exact spot where the owl first appeared. He swept his hand over Ellery's generous land, a gesture rich with love and knowledge, one he hoped a good man might recognize.

Solidarity
Is Not a Floor

FRANCINE LOVE,
student and community volunteer

On the first day of spring, Francine Love asks to
ride in to work with her father.

"What for?" he asks. He looks up from his
paper—not a regular newspaper, with the regular front-
page news of the strike, now in its fourteenth month.
No. Francine's father, who is trolling for tenure, takes *The
Chronicle of Higher Education* with his morning coffee.

"She doesn't need a reason, Bruce," Cindy says. "She's
your daughter, it's a Saturday, she'd like to ride in with
you."

"I need something from the library," Francine explains.

Her father—not a papermaker, not on strike, not interested in matters of social justice except for the occasional policy change at Blaine College that might directly
affect him—says, "You're in the eighth grade, Francine.
What could you possibly need from a college library?"

"What does she have to do, Bruce?" Cindy asks. "Fill out an application? Take her, for crying out loud."

He looks annoyed, then ashamed. Francine is used to these rearrangements of his face. "Sure, all right," he says. "I'll take you in."

Francine pretends to forgive him, to have no idea why he wants to go to work on a Saturday.

It is noon, a soupy rain befalling the town, by the time they finally leave. Cindy waves from the doorway, haloed by fluffy, reddish-blond hair, so beautiful and sweet that Francine cannot imagine what in the world her father could still be looking for. They've been married three years—the best three years of Francine's life, so far.

"All buckled in," she says to her father, who has made no mention of safety.

Her father flings a hand through the shiny long waves of his hair and starts the car. "What's your report about?" he asks as they round the long, wet curve of River Road. It has been raining for days, the snow disappearing in gulps from the winter-weary woods. Across the foot-bridge, near the mill's south gate, Francine can just make out a group of picketers, quiet and tightly thronged in mid-shift. At shift change there will be more of them, to make a noisy gauntlet. She knows many of them by name.

"Jesse Jackson," she tells her father. "The Reverend Jesse Jackson."

Her father slides her a half-smile. "What is it, Black History Month at Abbott Falls Middle School?" He says this because there are no black people in Abbott Falls, a place where he is marking time, a very long time, it seems, until he can get seduced—that's the word he uses, *seduced*—away from this backwater to a place where you can get a decent latté and find somebody to hold a conversation with besides a papermaker with bad teeth.

"He's coming to speak to the strikers next week," Francine says. Her father's crack about white Abbott Falls feels like a prejudice all its own, a paradox she cannot articulate. It's true the strikers hate the black men who came up to take their jobs, but they hate the white ones, too. If there were vile words for being a white person, Francine is pretty sure she'd have heard some by now. In her father's talk, which is always smart and well-turned, she hears his desperation, his smallness. He likes to tell people he chose Abbott Falls because it is a real place inhabited by real people, but in truth he can't afford a house on College Row.

Francine grasps all this, fleetingly, in the grayish privacy of her own head, where she works out the problem of family as if it were algebra, coming up with formulas that work cleanly, both sides equal. But in practice the formulas don't hold, they never hold, they crumble into pieces so fine they can't be put back.

BLAINE COLLEGE, about forty miles and fifteen solar systems west of Abbott Falls, is a formidable stonemasoned sanctuary where sixteen hundred students study philosophy and art and rarely venture off campus. The library, where her father drops her off, reminds Francine of a castle—it even has a turret. It occurs to her that steady exposure to a place like this might have a tendency to make some people feel royal.

The librarian, the queen of the castle in a tight dress, wears a ceramic badge that says LIBRARIAN. "Call me Gloria," she tells Francine, then, leaning into a whisper: "I'm one of the few here who properly apprehend the full meaning of your father's gifts."

"Well, he's very frustrated," Francine agrees.

Gloria's peachy face hovers, composed and hopeful. "Yes, he is." She straightens up. "Let me grab the keys and I'll take you to AV."

Francine, stranded in the carpeted atrium, glances furtively around the library. Almost everyone here is white, as it turns out, despite her father's smirkiness about Abbott Falls. Through the window, across the soaked campus green, gallops a bronze-colored student with a letter jacket hunched over his head to combat the rain. Except for his color he looks a lot like those galootish full-backs on the Abbott Falls football team. She would like to find someone more stately, charismatic, possessed of a dignified anger, someone who can look at what he is seeing and express it exactly. Someone like the Reverend Jesse Jackson. She does spot one other black person, a girl slouched in a chair by the window, her hair smoothed into an old-fashioned pageboy. But she looks kind of dopey, maybe hungover, like a sorority sister who had a bad night, and she's talking to a white girl in dreadlocks with a jewel in her forehead. What does this mean?

In her head she calls him Jesse. Just plain Jesse. Her friend Jesse.

She has come here armed with the facts of his life: his illegitimate birth, his absent father, his Greenville childhood, his faultless forward march toward nobility. *I was born in the slum, but the slum was not born in me.* Into Jesse's childhood street, Haney Street (in which she pictures a lonely, gifted black boy, so lonely and searching), she has placed tin cans rattling mournfully in the gutter, a single broken streetlight, and two dogs that pack together, one black, one white—little Jesse's first metaphor. *We sit here together, a rainbow, a coalition....* She has acquired two photographs: one, the fragile Jesse, a little child with chestnut cheeks and parted hair; the other, the rakish preacher, broad shouldered and mustachioed, arms folded, an immaculate handkerchief triangled out from his breast pocket.

Gloria is back, rattling keys. "Now," she says, all business: "You wanted to see some footage?"

Francine nods, eyeing the stacks. "Whatever you have. I just want to hear him talk."

Gloria unlocks a room cluttered with sound and video equipment and leads Francine to a computer terminal. "Most of what we have is on CD," she explains, sitting Francine down and reaching over her to scroll through an index, then another, and another. Francine, who notes several shortcuts that Gloria either doesn't know or does not wish to take, waits patiently until Gloria finishes her orientation and leaves.

The first thing Francine notices, watching the screen version of her friend Jesse striding to the podium at the 1988 Democratic Convention, is that he walks like a man with no intention of ever stopping. It is almost a surprise when he does. His voice is melodic, with certain imperfections of speech, a stoppage here and there as certain syllables blot together. His mouth fills with poetry, then the poetry floats out, not perfectly. She is entranced. Although she has memorized whole sections of his speeches, and this speech in particular, Jesse's voice visits her as something both familiar and strange, as if she'd stepped into her morning shower and out poured gold dust, or feathers, or butterflies. Francine does not understand that she is falling, that Jesse Jackson is the first in what will be a series of miserable crushes, that when the news of Jesse's love child breaks two years hence, she will be sick with betrayal. Instead, she feels as if she is rising. Rising toward knowledge. She waits for the feeling to pass, and mercifully, it doesn't. By the time Jesse Jackson lifts his chin and exhorts his listeners to "keep hope alive, keep hope alive, keep hope alive," she believes he is talking directly to her.

Her father does not turn up at the appointed time, so Francine takes in Jesse's speeches again, each one of them, before turning in the disks, thanking Gloria, and crossing the soggy campus. Though she thinks rarely of her mother, who lives in London and hates rain, this kind of weather does bring her to mind. She clops over the granite steps of the art building, which is smallish, old, one of the last to merit renovation. It smells of turpentine and other chemicals, and also of must and ancient wood and a different century. She climbs the worn stairs to the third floor, fearful of finding something she has not heretofore imagined in any detail, but when she creeps down the hall, past the splattered art rooms to her father's gloomy office, she finds the door ajar and her father alone at his desk. He gets up when he sees her and gathers his things. "Finished already?" he asks.

Francine just stands there. "You said four. It's five-thirty."

He makes a show of inspecting his watch. He taps it a few times, as if Francine is too young to tell time and cannot see that his watch is fine. "Well, kiddo," he says, "I guess it's time to go."

His closed briefcase sits upon his desk. There are two coffee cups, one half-drunk, the other full, on a table by the one window. He has a couch in there. It is then she sees the girl, so dark in the murk of her father's office that at first glance she appears one with the long, soft drape. Their eyes lock. Her face is angled, plum-colored, her lips billowed and shiny, her irises a rich, compelling shade of amber. She steps into the room, revealing herself, and her father says, "This is Shaleese," as if he were introducing someone from the office next door. The girl nods, then leaves, her hair rattling with beads. Francine listens to the rattling echo: *tapa-tapa-tapa-tapa-tapa*. Down one flight, *tapa-tapa-tapa-tapa*, down the next flight, *tapa-tapa-tapa*, fainter now, like a far-off musical instrument, an instrument used for sending signals, fainter and fainter, then the soft hush of a door.

Her father grabs his briefcase, cool, offhand, lips pursed. He touches the small of her back and hustles her out the door. On the way downstairs, he asks, "So, kiddo, get lots of info on Dr. King?"

"Yeah," she says. "Lots." Outside the sky has cleared.

It seems impossible that the bloated clouds have disintegrated in so short a time, and yet they have, leaving an ordinary late-afternoon sky, low-lit and clear, as if it had not rained at all.

They get into the car and head home. Her father is talking, but Francine's head fills with Jesse's voice, grand and comforting. *I understand. I know abandonment.* Jesse's passion makes her feel enfolded, taken in, thrillingly blue-collar. For a moment the contrast is such that she imagines she hates her father. But the ride home is long and quiet, and by the time they reach Abbott Falls, her hate has dissolved into the usual yearning, that soft, monotonous ache, like a bruise that keeps getting whacked afresh.

ON MONDAY afternoon, last period, Mrs. Therriault, whose husband is the treasurer of Local 20, gives Francine an A on the spot, casting a disapproving eye over Francine's classmates, who have done run-of-the-mill reports on historical figures like Paul Revere. Francine is glad enough to get the A, but the public nature of her triumph is bound to strain her relationship with her classmates, which isn't very chummy to begin with.

"You will note Francine's emphasis on the Reverend Jackson's efforts on behalf of the American labor movement," Mrs. Therriault informs the class. Her glasses slide down her long nose, giving her the appearance of an educated giraffe. "Very timely, considering his forthcoming visit." Francine leans forward, hoping for another of Mrs.

T's pro-union diatribes, which she finds enthralling. Mrs. T, however, has been informally enjoined from expressing in-class opinions about Atlantic Pulp & Paper—a clear violation of her civil rights, she announced to the class a month ago, and that was the last she was going to say about the matter.

Now it seems she is about to disobey her gag order. She gathers herself, sliding her glasses back up. Most of the kids look eager. Not Cora Spencer, whose father and aunt crossed the picket line; not Marty Fallon, whose mother manages Laverdiere's Drug and was the one to complain about Mrs. T's current-events lessons. "I hope you will all turn out next Saturday for the Reverend's speech," she intones, "a speech that is sure to soothe the heart of many a foot soldier in the war against—"

The next words—*the corporate barracudas whose jagged teeth have bitten into the very flesh of our community*—remain unspoken. The class has heard this speech before. Mrs. T clears her throat, looks as martyred as possible, and finishes up: "Well. Heaven forbid I should violate any mandates." She folds her arms. "Thank you, Francine. And I hope the rest of you were listening for a change. Now. Chapter questions on the Constitution."

Francine goes for her book, but just then Mrs. T clears her throat again, loud. "Speaking of the Constitution," she says, leveling them with a look that could fell trees, "freedom of speech is a *right*. It's a *right*, people." She waits, tapping her pink fingernail against her teeth. "Well, guess what. I believe I've just had one of my ideas." Everyone in the class—not Cora Spencer, not Marty

Fallon—straightens up. Mrs. T notes the shift, then continues: "Consider for a moment the Reverend Jackson's special fondness for young people and his inspiring work on their behalf." She glares around, as if defying them to deny the frigid fact that young people are ingrates first and last. "Wouldn't it be wonderfully a propos if one of my young people introduced Reverend Jackson at the rally?"

Francine cannot believe what she is hearing. Mrs. T has a lot of influence—Francine has seen her at the union hall, grading papers and making picket signs simultaneously—and there is no question that her wish will be somebody's command. Already Francine imagines the surge of warmth as her friend Jesse enfolds her hand in his—the meeting of kindred spirits. Already she imagines adjusting her glasses, evening up her note cards, staring out at the multitude collected in the high school gym. Keep hope alive, she thinks. Her father will beam from the crowd, and Cindy, and Kenny (who's been nothing but kind since returning home); maybe they'll call London to let her mother know.

Face flaming, she looks up at Mrs. T. But Mrs. T is looking at Eddie Little. Everybody is looking at Eddie Little, son of Roy Little, president of Local 20. Francine has just given a report on the Reverend Jesse Jackson, has delivered a pitch-perfect imitation of his famous lines, but still everybody is looking at Eddie Little.

Then Mrs. T snaps up a notepad and aims her pen. "Let's get a ballpark on how many of you would like to be considered for the privilege." Three hands shoot up, three volunteers, three combatants: Francine, Eddie, and Meghan Bouvier, who is beautiful, period, and has won every single thing she has ever competed for. Except this time. She wonders if Meghan will mind. If it hurts more to lose if you never lose.

"Fine," Mrs. T says, scribbling the names on a pad. "Tomorrow. Two-minute practice intro from each of you. The class will vote." Most of the time she treats the class like feeble-minded inmates, except for the times, as now, when she treats them like game-show contestants.

When the end-of-day bell rings, Francine marshals her courage and waylays Eddie Little at his locker. "I'm very qualified," she says, her body humming with panic; she fears her lips may tremble clean off her face. "You heard my report, right?"

Eddie looks at her, registering surprise. She has never spoken to him outside of class, though he was her peer reviewer for language-arts last fall. *Good similars*, he'd written on her poem, a long rhyming poem called "The Fifteen Fingers of Freedom." Eddie is tall and well-liked. He plays basketball and this is a basketball town. Some of the other kids have stopped to gawk, and Francine feels like a big, ugly toad-person, a slug-person, a creature made of fat and slime.

"You're not even *from* here," Eddie says.

"My mother is," Francine says, then corrects herself: "My stepmother." She remembers, a second too late, that Cindy was once married to Eddie's uncle. That Cindy broke Eddie's uncle's heart into about four million pieces.

Eddie blinks at her. "She's not from here, either," he says, meaning: Not a mill family.

This is the worst thing you can say in this town, at this time.

"She grew up right on Lincoln Street," Francine says, suddenly enraged on Cindy's behalf. "She's your *aunt.*"

"Not anymore," Eddie informs her. But he is not a mean boy—there are mean boys in this school, and Eddie Little is not one of them—so he knocks her gently on the shoulder and says, "May the best man win."

Which allows Francine to flee the hallway still in possession of a shred of dignity. This is the first time she has been touched by a boy. For this she will be grateful to Eddie Little, she is sure, all her life.

When Francine arrives at the union hall on the following Saturday, two hours early for Jesse's arrival, something is wrong. The usual people are there: Eddie's father, Roy Little; three of Eddie's uncles, including the one whose heart Cindy broke; Mrs. Therriault's husband, talking on the phone with his face afire; Allan Landry, in his too-small T-shirt, belly half-mooning above his belt; and about twenty more of the inside circle, everybody talking at once, low and secret and disbelieving.

There has been bad news.

Two other phones are ringing and nobody answers. Voices crack and thunk, the phone ringing over them.

Francine sets to work, trying to make herself both useful and inconspicuous. She joins two women boxing food at a long table. "What's going on?" she asks, grabbing an empty crate.

One of the women is old, the other just looks old. The old woman—a parishioner from St. Anne's—shakes her head. "Maybe Jackson canceled, is all I can think of."

The other woman—a lean, leathery striker whom Francine has seen shrieking on the gauntlet—lifts her chin. "Big surprise," she mutters. She picks up a canned ham and looks at it. She wants it.

"He wouldn't cancel," Francine says, eyeing the ham. "Jesse would never do that."

"Right," the woman says. "They're so famous for keeping their word."

An uncomfortable silence descends upon them. The old woman pretends not to have heard. *Thwuk, thwuk, thwuk*, goes the food into the boxes. The leathery woman's bunions, pink and bare, poke out from the ripped uppers of her sneakers.

Francine moves away, down the length of the table where she can work alone. She boxes up a couple of cans of soup, some spaghetti sauce, tins of cat food and tuna fish, some toilet paper: a little of everything necessary to get through a day without crossing over. The box will be delivered without fanfare, anonymously, to a striker family with no second income and a cleaned-out savings account. When she peers sideways at the women, she catches the leathery woman, whose bunions must be cold, staring at the older woman's hair, which has just been permed. Not everybody has suffered equally. At first everybody was equally angry, their anger a straight, perfectly directed line, like an electrical current running from Abbott Falls, Maine, to the headquarters of Atlantic Pulp & Paper in New York City. Now the long months have intervened. Their anger is no longer perfect. It is less an electrical current than a lightning bolt, jagged and hard to control and not as fussy about its target.

How many times in these long months have those two women stood here, on what Ray Little calls this hallowed floor? What have they really been thinking? *Solidarity forevvver, solidarity forevvver,* they have sung many times, standing on this hallowed floor: *The union makes us stronnng!* Francine loves that song, she hums it all the time. But solidarity is not a floor, she has found. It is a ladder. People end up on different rungs.

She lifts a crate of oranges and divvies them up. Along the upper balcony of the cavernous room—a century ago it was a grange hall, and it still seems suited to farmers gathering to talk prices and play mandolins—she can see Roy Little pacing frantically, arms flying, in a wide blade of light from a partly open door. Mrs. T isn't here tonight, but her husband is, slamming down a phone and yelling something across to Allan Landry.

Something awful has happened; the women sense it, too. They stop, looking upward.

Eddie is in there, Francine sees, the only other kid in the place, because he has been chosen to deliver Jesse's introduction. Meghan Bouvier got six votes and Eddie got the remaining nineteen. Eddie and Meghan voted for each other and Francine voted for Eddie. He leaps out of the office and tears down the stairs, weaving his way through snags of chairs, tables laden with clothes, food, brochures, lumber, sheets of cardboard.

Francine steels herself: "What happened?" she calls to him. She doesn't want it to be that Jesse canceled; she doesn't want that poor woman with her bunions to be right.

Eddie looks at her, hesitates, then walks over, flush with news. "They're folding up shop. McCoy and them. It's over."

McCoy means Henry John McCoy, CEO of Atlantic Pulp & Paper. The rest she does not understand. The women have already headed up the stairs, mouths working. Francine looks helplessly at Eddie.

"They're putting the mill up for sale," Eddie explains, slowly, as if speaking to an imbecile. But he looks frightened. "It's over."

"The strike's over?" Francine says, not believing. "The strike's over?"

Eddie grimaces. "*Everything's* over. McCoy's firing the scabs after tonight's shift." He looks at her, his blue eyes intent. "We're not strikers anymore. We're just working stiffs at a plant closing."

Though she understands that Eddie has just snatched those words from his father, she envies him the word *we*. "What about Jesse?" Francine asks. "Is he still coming?"

Eddie snorts. "Yeah. A lotta good it'll do now." Then he wings past her, probably fetching something for his father, something important and secret.

Word has gone out, instantly, the way it always does. People arrive in small, panicky surges. Some of the men start putting chairs in place. There will be a makeshift meeting before the rally. Francine races over to the coffeemaker, pours a cup for Roy—cream and two sugars, this is how he takes it—and climbs to the inner sanctum with the cup proffered. Roy, engulfed by questions, his shirt sweat-stained, crumpled by worry, spots her and yells over a clanging phone: "Will somebody get that kid out of here?"

Somebody—a woman, someone she doesn't know—takes Francine gently by the shoulders and guides her out the door. "Not now, dear," she says, as if Francine were an orphaned animal she had to be kind to. Francine shrinks into the doorway, recognizing the tone as the one her father takes most of the time, and her teachers, and even some of the nicer girls in her class.

It is over. It is all collapsing as she stands there with an unwanted coffee. A couple of reporters, jackets flaring, enter the hall, a news truck pulls up in front, word is spreading like an oil spill in this town she does not belong to. Today's news is one of those turning points—there have been so many! fourteen months!—that will bring back the national news people, their cigarette-smoking cameramen and boom operators and anchorpeople in makeup, some important and some not, you can tell by who jumps when who snaps. And Francine will not be interviewed for anything, will be passed over in any crowd she places herself in, for she is not informed, not pretty, not from here. Jesse will be arriving soon, altering his poetry on the fly, speaking not to righteous strikers but to dazed, defeated workers who have just been slapped into the street. Jesse is good at this; his speech will be recorded and shown, his show of solidarity. *I understand.* Even the woman with bunions, her eyes will fill. Jesse will come here, slip out of his jacket, pull one of those red T-shirts over his bleached white shirt. He will speak. They will listen. *Hold your head high, stick your chest out. You can make it.* They will believe, Yes, we can. We can make it. And Francine will squeeze and shuffle toward the front, where he will fail to notice her, where his eyes will pass over the professor's daughter with a fax machine in her bedroom who has not known a moment's deprivation, not one, since the day she was born.

It is all collapsing. She spies Eddie rabbitting back and forth, vibrating with responsibility. The place balloons with news, with people, with a muted, unappealing hybrid of despair and resentment that Francine has not sensed before. She can almost smell it. And because she has no claim on the thing that is collapsing, Francine slips into the street and heads into the teeming evening with the coffee cup still in her hand.

It takes her a long time to get home. She stops every so often just to listen to the faraway hissing of the mill, to watch the last of the smoke and steam. By the time she reaches her white house on the corner of Randall and Pine, it is time for the rally. She listens, and fancies she can barely make out crowd sounds. She puts the cup under the hedge and goes in.

Because Francine's real mother has been gone a very long time, finding Cindy in the kitchen at the end of a day is like crashing through a bramble and happening upon a tame deer. Her father was better before Cindy came—home more, nicer—but she prefers Cindy to anything her father used to be. Because of this, she is careful. She tries to be only smart, only cooperative, only wanted.

"I thought you were going to the rally," Cindy says, looking up from a sweater she's trying to pull a thread back into.

"I decided not to."

Cindy puts the sweater down. "Francine, you've talked of nothing else for a week. You were hell-bent on shaking Jesse Jackson's hand."

Francine digs her fingernails hard into her wrist to keep from crying. It works. "I figured I'd see him easier on TV," she lies. "There's about a million people."

"Then let's turn it on," Cindy says, dropping everything. She switches on the public-access channel and sits next to Francine. The gym looks thronged and noisy. Roy Little gets up, takes too long to adjust the squalling mic, then delivers the bad news.

"Oh, my God," Cindy says. She looks at Francine. "Did you know this?"

Francine nods, listens some more to Roy. They're going to sue for back wages, pension packages, sick time, vacation. Then he introduces Jesse; with a stab of satisfaction Francine realizes that in the developing news Eddie has lost his privilege. She looks for him in the crowd, but he is lost in there.

Then it is Jesse's turn. Francine cannot bear to look at him. It is a feeling like grief, seeing her friend who does not know her. Who does not know what that woman said today in the union hall. As she predicted, his poetry elicits a swell of affirmation from the crowd. Listening to him feels exactly like listening to her mother's staticky London voice on the phone: the voice is far away, familiar solely to the imagination, and tendered through a scrim of theater.

Wherever you are tonight, you can make it.

"Yes," Francine murmurs, as if answering the preacher in Jesse's childhood church.

You can make it.

"Yes."

It gets dark sometimes, but the morning comes.

"Yes, it gets dark sometimes, but the morning comes."

The rally goes long, with lots of singing, and shouting, and crying, and then everybody spills into the night, where they will march over to the mill gates. Some will stand mute and stolid, signs raised over their heads; some will kick doors and punch windshields. This is always how it goes.

Cindy shakes her head. She slides her arm behind Francine's shoulders and gives her a squeeze. "Sweet Jesus," she says. "I thought this town couldn't get any bleaker, but I guess I was wrong." She sighs, getting up. "You need anything, Francine? I'm going to make some phone calls."

"No."

"All right, then," she says, then pads off to her bedroom.

Francine's father does not arrive until late in the late news, which shows highlights of Jesse's speech but manages to thwart the flow, the poetry, the presence. She hears her father in the kitchen: freezer door, ice tray, a glass taken down from the cabinet. He appears in the doorway and leans.

Francine mutes the television. "Did you hear?"

"Yeah," he says. "Tough break."

"Some people will make out all right," Francine says. "Some people started with more."

"Some people always do," he says. "Shouldn't you be in bed?" He swirls the drink in his hand, then sits next to her, which he never does. They watch the voiceless weatherman wave his hands in front of a satellite photo.

"Daddy?" Francine says.

Her father's head swivels toward her: she never calls him that.

"Does Cindy know?"

He takes a sip. "Does Cindy know what?"

"About that girl."

Another sip. "What girl?"

"That girl in your office. The girl with the . . . beads."

Her father arranges his face one way, then another. Francine stares him down, hoping he will not make up a story. What girl? Oh, her? My assistant? My colleague's daughter? That pain in the neck who came by to complain about her grade?

Francine waits. She is willing to wait.

"No," her father says, finally. "Cindy doesn't know."

The room seems to shrink around them, corralling a secret.

"Cindy will leave if she finds out," Francine says after a moment. The words freeze between them.

Her father jiggles his glass; the ice cubes sound like chattering teeth. He does not ask her not to tell. He knows she won't. He knows absolutely.

Now Francine gets up, rattled by an ambiguous gratitude, seduced by the notion that she, Francine Love, is a person about whom it is possible to have inside knowledge. That her father is the one who possesses it.

"Good night," she tells him, moving quickly up the stairs, hoping to be asleep before the feeling fades. Instead, she pauses, as she has on countless nights, in the shadowy hallway outside her father's bedroom. She covers her eyes with her fists to shut out the frightening dark. Listening hard, she hears it at last: the comfort of Cindy's slumber, those long, solid breaths, reliable and unaware.

Shuffle, Step

ERNIE WHITTEN, *retired pipefitter*

Five months to the day after Marie's passing, Ernie won free dance lessons in a raffle. He'd bought the ticket from a girl in the neighborhood raising money for her middle-school jazz band. There were other prizes on the list—movie passes, a year of bouquets from Showers of Flowers, and a month of lunches at the Libby Road Burger King—all of which assumed the presence of a partner. With Marie gone, Ernie saw the world more than ever as a place for two-by-two.

He had tried to explain this to the eighth-grader standing on his doorstep who introduced herself as Francine Love, but she merely shrugged her meaty shoulders and informed him, "You won't win, anyway." She was a round, soft girl with beach-colored hair cut straight off just below her ears. Her glasses were heavy and squarish, and she wore a big blue sweatshirt over big blue sweatpants. Ernie's son had been a child like this, inexplicably heart-breaking, out of step in ways hard to pin down. For her awful glasses alone, Ernie bought four books of tickets at five bucks a crack, enough, he figured, to finance a new reed for her saxophone.

And now here she was again, back on his doorstep, grinning at him through chapped lips, holding out a pink-and-white brochure for Melanie Bouchard's School of Dance at 425 West Main. Ernie's had been the fourth ticket drawn. Last prize, but a prize nonetheless, the only winning ticket Francine Love had ever sold in her eight-year school career.

"So we're both winners, in a way," she said.

Ernie took the brochure timidly, as if its folds might conceal a tiny, sharp-toothed animal. "Well," he said. "Thank you, then."

The girl was staring at him through her magnified green eyes, her whispery eyelashes brushing against the lenses. "Thank you, then, Francine," Ernie said again, hoping to hurry her along.

"It's an excellent school of dance," Francine proclaimed, nudging her chin toward the brochure. "Dancing is very good exercise, particularly for older people." Her eyes darted right, then left; she spotted Marie's Yorkie quaking in the sunporch behind him.

"Oh, what a *cute* little dog," Francine exclaimed. "Can I hold him?"

Ernie handed over the terrified dog, whereupon Francine proceeded to cuddle it close to her face and kiss its ears. The dog went limp with gratitude. "What's his name?" Francine asked. "He's so *cute*."

"Pumpkin Pie," Ernie said. "My wife named him."

"Hi, Pumpkie," Francine squealed, hugging the dog. "Hi, Pumpkie-boy-boy."

Ernie allowed the girl to go on for a few moments, for this is exactly how Marie had handled the dog, all this cooing and carrying on, and he figured the poor beast missed a woman's voice in its wiry ears. When she was done, Francine said, "You're not going to take the dance class, are you."

"Well, no," Ernie admitted. "I'm no dancer." When she didn't leave, he added, "If that's all right."

Francine petted the dog absently. She began to look around at Ernie's yard, the empty bird feeders, the untended grass. It was May, and Marie's wildflowers were beginning to dot the lawn. Inevitably Francine's gaze fixed upon the ark Ernie had built in his first and only fit of artistic inspiration, one that had come to him—from God, he believed now—during the last lucid weeks of Marie's cancer. He'd swaddled his dying wife on the sunporch so she could watch him prove he was a man who could still see the possibility in a blank board. Over the years he'd built furniture for her, and birdhouses, and a new bathroom, and the sunporch, but the ark was a mystery that only after her passing he'd recognized as a monument to her, a vessel that contained her last weeks, which had been filled with entertainment and unseasonable weather and the joyful *ping* of hammer on nail.

"I watched you build that boat," Francine said.

"Ark," Ernie corrected her. "It was an artistic inspiration."

"I knew that," Francine said. "Everybody wondered what the heck you were doing. You know what I told them?"

"I can't say as I do."

"I told them creativity can't be thwarted." She blinked a few times. "That's what our band director always says. He's an extremely smart man."

Ernie pondered this for a moment. "My wife liked it," he said. The ark's shadow covered most of the lawn at this time of day, he was surprised to notice; though it was broad and hulking and a story high, Ernie could go days without seeing it at all.

"You've let it go," Francine said. "You've got chipmunks and things in there."

"So did Noah."

Francine didn't laugh. "All my family felt bad about your wife," she said. "She was a nice person to see around the neighborhood." She pointed down the street. "I live over there."

He looked at the white house on the corner. He'd lost track of most of the neighbors over the years; he was not, as Marie always put it, a "mixer."

"Did you get our card?"

Ernie nodded, though in truth he had yet to open any of the cards that had come in, many from people Ernie didn't know well: people from Marie's book group, from the library where she'd worked for years, from neighbors and acquaintances who had been Marie's domain. Marie had been the one in charge of friendships, and he couldn't imagine what comfort her friends' words might provide now.

"Anyway," Francine went on, "my question is, is it still a winning ticket if the winner doesn't claim the prize?"

"But I don't have the time to claim it," Ernie said. "My

son's coming out from California to visit. You could give the prize to somebody else."

Francine thought this over. "When does your son get here?"

Ernie sensed a trap but stepped right in, mostly because Marie's dog looked as if it had been born in Francine's arms. "Saturday," he allowed.

"The lesson's on Friday," Francine said. "Your son won't even be here yet." Her face stilled, and Ernie saw that this girl was like everyone else in this town—fixed on the smallest triumphs, undone by losses they could neither identify nor comprehend. Probably her only girlfriend had moved away, or her parents had broken up, or there was an uncle or cousin who'd crossed the picket line. Although Ernie, whose retirement date had fallen three weeks after the mill went out on strike, should have been as affected as anyone by the strike's ache and duration and violence, Marie's cancer had kept him in a strangely comforting netherworld. It wasn't until after she died that he looked around the town he'd lived in all his life and could not believe what he saw.

"You don't have to have a partner, Mr. Whitten," Francine said. "If that's what you're worried about."

"Oh, well," Ernie said, "that's not—"

"Mr. Whitten," Francine said, "it would mean a real, real lot to me if you claimed your prize." She put the dog down. "We could go together."

In this manner, the matter was settled. A simple request from a neighbor girl, the first request from any human being since Marie's breathless "Hold me, Ernie," when he'd felt what was left of her lift from the earth and dissolve into stars.

FRANCINE STOPPED in at five-thirty on Friday evening with her dance shoes stowed into a plastic grocery bag that dangled from her wrist. She was wearing the same blue sweatpants she'd had on when she first sold him the ticket, plus an oversized T-shirt emblazoned with SOLIDARITY FOREVER in red letters.

"The deal went through this morning," Francine said. "Did you hear that?"

Ernie nodded. Atlantic Pulp & Paper had been bought out by Global Paper Products, a South African firm that promised to have the plant up and running within weeks, honoring back wages and pension packages and seniority. It was as if the town of Abbott Falls, Maine, had won the raffle of raffles, but the whiff of despair and burned bridges had settled so far into the valley that it would be a long time before anyone felt like dancing. No one liked the idea of being bailed out by foreigners, of course, but there were other, worse things: too many who had said and done what they were now ashamed of; too many families ripped apart by money and rage; too many faces with similar features had foamed at one another from opposite sides of the gauntlet over too many shift changes. A year ago there might have been a mass celebration, people kissing in the streets as at the end of a war, an unleashing of church bells, but it was too late now; what Ernie sensed, taking the town's measure, was an oddly calibrated resignation, a triumph with most of the satisfaction scoured clean off it.

"Are you glad to be going back to work?" Francine asked.

"I'm not going," Ernie told her. "I'm retired. I'll be getting a check, if they mean what they say."

"They do," Francine assured him.

The evening was cool and dreamy, and their steps made bright, clopping sounds on the sidewalk as Ernie escorted Francine to 425 West Main. Melanie Bouchard's School of Dance, which in all these years Ernie had taken no notice of whatsoever, spanned the upper floors of Dave's Diner and Showers of Flowers. In the florist's window, as in many storefronts throughout town, hung a computer-generated banner wishing a warm welcome to Global Paper and a warmer welcome-back to the striking papermakers. The proprietress of Showers of Flowers, whose cheerful demeanor Ernie remembered as a comfort while arranging for Marie's funeral, had festooned her storefront with flowers made of bone-white, coated paper—a specialty of the Abbott Falls mill. "That's clever," Ernie said.

"My stepmother owns that shop," Francine informed him. "She's a very beautiful person."

Francine didn't appear to require an answer, so Ernie remained silent.

"She's so beautiful people buy flowers just to look at her face," Francine went on. Her voice dropped. "My father doesn't appreciate her at all. He has girlfriends I'm not supposed to know about." Between the shops was a narrow door with stenciled letters reading DANCE UPSTAIRS. "Here goes nothing," Francine said, flinging open the door.

Despite his misgivings, Ernie felt momentarily relieved to have something to take his mind away from his son's impending visit. It would be a typically quick visit, a two-day detour from doing business down in Portland for his new computer company; still, Ernie had written some topics on a note card in case they ran out of conversation. He no longer had Marie to take up the slack.

He followed Francine up the stairs, but to his confusion they led to a hallway in which people of varying ages and shapes were seated on benches, putting on tap shoes or taking them off. Some were teenaged girls wearing leotards cut embarrassing low in some places and embarrassingly high in others. There were a couple of women Ernie guessed to be young mothers getting out of the house, and a covey of slightly older women who looked like schoolteachers. There was only one other man, whom Ernie recognized as the assistant manager of Laverdiere's Drug on East Main. Slim and well-appointed as an expensive pencil, he came out of the studio with his face flaming from exertion and his shiny wingtips tapping merrily. Francine, who had put on a pair of black dance slippers, placed a reassuring hand on Ernie's arm. "He's in Advanced. You don't have to get taps right off."

Ernie looked around, adrenaline washing hotly through him. "I thought this was a *dance* lesson," he said. "Fox-trots and rumbas and what have you."

"Melanie doesn't teach ballroom," Francine said. "It's tap and jazz only. Jazz was full, and anyway, that's Tuesday nights. I have band practice." She pulled gently on his arm. "Come on."

Following Francine down the hallway, Ernie felt hapless, weirdly cornered, like a squirrel accepting a hand-feeding against all its inborn proclivities. They waited in line while a splendidly proportioned woman at a check-in table—Melanie Bouchard, presumably— took either money or punch cards from each prospective dancer, then punched cards or gave change and shooed them on. After giving Melanie ten dollars for her own lesson, Francine plunked down her half of Ernie's raffle ticket. "Here's my winner, Melanie," she said, presenting Ernie as if he himself were the prize. "He's free."

Melanie wrote Ernie's name on a list, then smiled hard at him, her rouged lips parting to show her big, frightening teeth. Her crimson leotard looked like something borrowed from a circus. "Congratulations, Mr. Whitten," Melanie said. "Welcome to Adult Tap." She pulled out a brand-new punch card, popped a fresh hole into its pink smoothness, and handed it to Ernie, who felt at this point the way he had back in Korea, engulfed by forces beyond his control.

He trailed Francine into the studio, watching dumbly as the beginners' class assembled: three of the women from the hallway, plus Francine. And Ernie himself. Some music came on, evenly measured, heavy-handed piano music that appeared to have been produced by a talented hippopotamus. Then Melanie clicked into the room and instructed the class to stand facing an unforgiving wall of mirrors.

"Fa-*lap*!" she called out, and produced an odd little

hiccup with her feet, which were encased in glossy red tap shoes with a high heel and ankle strap. Despite his complete mortification, Ernie could not help but admire the way Melanie held her arms away from her body, the comely turn of her ankle, the way her long neck lifted. "Fa-*lap*," she repeated. "Like *this*."

Ernie stood mute as a totem as Melanie demonstrated flaps and flap-heels and ball-changes and pull-backs and shuffles. His classmates imitated her with a mighty earnestness, their mismatched timing making the scene in the mirror resemble a calliope with different-colored animals moving up and down. Francine, who moved like a stalled snowplow, kept glancing at him sideways. Her arms stuck straight out from her sides, and with each connection of toe to floor, her body pitched forward from the waist. Ernie began to move his feet out of pity, surprised by the rhythm his body was able to keep. Fa-*lap*, ball-*change*, fa-*lap*, ball-*change*. Of course, he wished to go home, but more than that he wished to go home to Marie.

"Good!" Melanie called out. "Aaand! Shuffle! Like this!" And it was on to shuffle-hop-step, Ernie's classmates resuming their calliope imitation; Ernie, in his brown pants and shirt and shoes, felt like the ugly carnival man running the machine. "Aaaand," Melanie foamed, "shuffle-hop-step! Shuffle-hop-step! That's called an Irish, class—you're dancing!" As a reward Melanie sent them to the barre, where they did twenty minutes of drills that left Ernie's calves feeling profoundly insulted. Melanie clapped her hands and pronounced them the best darned beginners it had ever been her privilege to meet.

Ernie waited in the hallway while Francine changed her shoes, then escorted her down the stairs and into the street. They were both a little out of breath, and didn't talk until they'd reached the end of West Main and rounded the corner onto River.

"I took lessons when I was eight," Francine said. "I forgot everything."

Ernie glanced down at her—she came only to his shoulder, and he was not a tall man. "Why didn't you keep up your lessons?" he asked.

She shrugged. "Too fat."

Ernie had been hoping for a longer, more elaborate explanation that might get them as far as Elm, at least. He had never been good at talking to children, including his own son, and didn't expect much in the way of divine intervention at this late date. James had last visited in December—it wasn't a visit, it was Marie's funeral—and they'd mostly sat around the house in Marie's chairs not talking about her.

"We made enough on the raffle to send ten kids to band camp," Francine said.

"Congratulations," he said. She had big, bloomy cheeks, he noticed, the only truly childlike thing about her. "When do you go?"

She rolled her eyes. "I'm not going. There's about four million saxophonists better than me."

They made their way along the river, where the mill, having lain dormant for months, suddenly looked newly minted. A few cars dotted the parking lot, and people were moving in and out of the administrative offices. The waning sun banked off its brick sides, leaving an auburn burnish that Ernie hoped bespoke better times ahead.

"Here you are, Mr. Whitten," she said as they reached Ernie's gate. It needed paint, he noticed. Francine was smiling like a camp counselor after a successful sing-along. "You've got five lessons left," she reminded him. "Five Fridays."

"I was under the impression it was only the one," Ernie said. "That the one lesson was the prize. A very nice prize indeed."

"She gave you a punch card," Francine said. "It's a whole class, six weeks." She put her hands on her hips. "I'll take you to every one of them. If you want."

"I expect I can finish up by myself," said Ernie, who intended to do no such thing.

"I was watching you," she said. "You could be good. You can tell by the way a dancer holds himself." Another optimist, Ernie thought: Marie had believed the best of everyone, even the doctor who had twice pronounced her cured. Francine stuck out her hand, which was uncommonly soft. "Thank you for winning," she said. "Could I come visit your dog sometime?"

"I don't see why not. He certainly seems to like you."

"Animals do," she said, then sauntered off toward home, the plastic bag swinging from her wrist.

Ernie let the dog out and made a tour around the ark. Francine was right, he had let it go. He'd left the bare wood to the elements, and the boards had lifted in places, revealing tufts of leaf and grass dragged in there by small determined animals; but he knew what it once had been and meant, and tonight that felt like enough. He sat on the gangplank with the dog in his lap, thinking of the tap dancers he and Marie used to admire on *Ed Sullivan* or *Lawrence Welk*, impeccably costumed black men with furrowed brows and all their teeth showing, their shoes sparking against a shiny floor. What struck Ernie now, in the retrospect of this evening, was their self-containment. They were not top-hatted show-offs sweeping beautiful women across yards of stage; they were tap dancers, confined to a spotlight-sized circle made large by virtue of their modest, tippy-tapping pleasure. Every last one of them must have started with a simple fa-*lap*.

Out on the street, cars began to cruise by. There was a subtle form of celebration going on after all, bands of people arriving at one doorstep or another. A cautious resurrection, Ernie thought: their rejoicing had a manufactured quality, as if they were so out of practice they'd had to consult a manual.

After supper Ernie found the stack of unopened cards and selected the one with the Loves' return address. It was signed *From your neighbors, the Loves, with our sympathy* in a woman's hand, and beneath that, in what Ernie took to be Francine's eighth-grade scrawl: *She was a nice person to see around the neighborhood.* Ernie closed the card, then read the others. There were some nice remembrances, and he was glad to have them, and surprised to be glad. He collected the cards and put them on the kitchen table for James to read the next day. Then he remembered that James had once liked fudge, so he took sugar and chocolate from the cupboard and set to work.

*   *   *

JAMES ARRIVED around lunchtime, knocking at the little-used front door just as Francine, holding a leash with the price tag still attached, rang the bell on the side. Ernie let his son in first; then, glad for something to do, hurried through the kitchen and into the sunporch to greet Francine. Once he had them both in his kitchen, he didn't know what to do with either one of them.

"I thought the town was after you to take that thing down," James said, gesturing out the window toward Ernie's ark.

"They sent a fellow out here two or three times, but he kept losing the citations and what have you."

"Creativity can't be thwarted," Francine said. She already had the dog in her arms. "Is that fudge?"

"Have some," Ernie urged them both.

"I'm on a diet," James said, then sat heavily at the kitchen table. Ernie regarded his son, who had not aged well. His hair was thin as a baby's and he had a babyish roll of fat around his waist. He'd inherited nothing from his mother except her smile, which he rarely used.

"Chocolate adds years to your life," Francine declared. "They did studies."

James looked at her.

"Francine knows everything," Ernie explained.

James took a piece of fudge and chewed it thoughtfully. He looked at the stack of sympathy cards on the table. "How are you, Dad?" he asked wearily.

"He's fine. He's a winner," Francine said, hooking the leash to the dog's collar. "Can I take Pumpkie-boy for a walk?"

"Sure," Ernie said.

"A really long one? Like down to the mill and back?"

"Anywhere you want," Ernie said, and watched as she trotted off, the dog following, obedient as a pull-toy.

James cleared his throat. "She's a strange one." Ernie shrugged.

"You were like that."

"I don't think I went around haunting the neighbors," James said, then smiled after all, a flash of Marie passing between them.

"Actually," Ernie said, "you did." He sat down. "How's Carrie?" He instantly regretted this blunder: James's daughter, now nineteen, was the type of girl they used to call "wayward."

"Last I heard," James said, "she was in Seattle." There was more, Ernie guessed—with Carrie there always was—but he was in no position to ask. He sensed that his son could use some advice, the grandfather's perspective—but he didn't know his granddaughter well and hadn't spoken to her since Marie died.

"I've been looking at condos," James said.

Ernie picked up the saltshaker and rolled it in his palms. "I thought you liked where you were, son." He blushed; the word *son* sounded hammy and wrong, as if he were auditioning for a part in a family movie.

James looked up. "Not for me. For you. They have these retirement communities."

"You mean in San Francisco?"

"Walnut Creek," James said. "I'd be a stone's throw away." His voice was heavy with obligation, rich with it.

"I'm sixty-five years old, James," Ernie said. "I've got better things to do than play bingo with a bunch of people who can't remember what work is."

"What are you so busy doing?" James asked, gesturing around the kitchen, which did need a cleaning. "It doesn't seem like you're exactly thriving."

Ernie sat back, folding his arms, eyeing his son. He didn't want to argue with him, for with Marie gone there was no telling what they might say. He missed her acutely, her influence, the way she softened the edges of everything. "You're in this house ten minutes and you've got the picture, is that it?"

"I thought you'd be relieved," James said. He turned his blue eyes—he'd always had frank, appraising eyes—toward Ernie. "Do you have friends?" He seemed embarrassed to have to ask.

"I've lived here all my life," Ernie said, which did not, he knew, answer his son's question. "I have friends," he added, but in truth he could think of only two right off the bat: one was dead and the other was going on fourteen years old. He was angry with James, mostly because it was true: he'd been here ten minutes and gotten the picture.

"What do you do all day?" James asked rhetorically. "Where do you go?"

"As a matter of fact," Ernie said, "I seem to have taken up tap dancing."

James looked as if Ernie had just announced his candidacy for governor. "It's excellent exercise," Ernie went on, "especially for older people."

"Tap dancing?" James said. "Seriously?"

"I won lessons. Francine sold me the ticket."

James looked as if he might want to smile, then didn't. "I don't believe you," he said.

Ernie got up slowly and showed his son a shuffle-hop-step. He bit his tongue gently, concentrating. "They call that an Irish," he said. "I'm not selling this place."

James looked exhausted and confused. His suit was travel-rumpled, his fragile hair mashed down on one side, and his eyelids had begun to thicken with age. James's life was not easy, Ernie knew. He spent most of every day in a car; he lived in a place where fat men did not do well; he'd sired a daughter who courted trouble; he'd married a woman who did not adore him. Ernie himself had had a far easier time of things. "I'm trying to do something right for a change," James said quietly. "It's a little late, I know."

"Well, I don't need taking care of. You can rest easy on that score." Ernie put his hands on the table, flat down, thinking he might slide them over, but instead he picked up the sympathy cards and placed them into a neat stack. "It's not your fault we're like this, son." There it was again, that word; he could not stop saying it.

James wiped his face hard with his hands. He stared at the cards on the table. "I think of her a lot, Dad. I hope you know that."

Ernie had always thought of his son as cold, but here, now, in his soft, travel-worn clothes, he did not seem cold at all. He watched as James leafed through the cards.

"These are nice," his son said. "Thanks for getting them out."

Ernie shrugged. "I just got down to opening them myself yesterday."

James didn't look surprised. He took off his sports jacket and hung it on the chair-back. This took almost a minute. There was nothing else to say, and two days to fill, and Ernie's feeling of burden doubled with the knowledge that his son felt the same way.

"I'll tell you what you can do for me," Ernie said, getting up. It felt good just to move. The air stirred, and that was something. "You said you wanted to do something. Well, I've got something, if you meant what you said."

James looked up, apprehensive. "I meant what I said."

"You can help me fix up the ark."

James seemed bewildered. "The front steps are a mess," he said. "Your gutters are clogged, the garage needs painting. If we're going to do a fix-up, Dad, there are a hundred other places to start."

"You want to do something, this is the thing needs doing," Ernie said. "Your mother'd have a cow if she could see how I let the thing go." He took his cap from a peg next to the kitchen door. "You in or out?" He lingered at the door, feeling suspended, waiting for his son.

James got up reluctantly, picking up his jacket. "All right. Sure. I'm in, sure."

"I thought maybe we take the table saw up from the basement," Ernie said. "Rip us some batten strips out there in the sunshine, cover those gaps." Time loosened just then; the millions of stalled minutes since Marie's passing stuttered open. "You'll need some easier clothes," he told his son.

They set up in the yard with some fudge, a bite of lunch, and the table saw. Ernie ripped a series of strips and handed them up to James, who stood on a ladder in Ernie's clothes.

When Francine came back with the dog, she un-hooked the leash and placed it on the sunporch steps in a neat coil. She stepped into the unmowed grass, looking at them. "I'm finishing the dance lessons, Mr. Whitten," she yelled over the whining saw. "My stepmother gave me the money." Then, to James: "How long are you staying?"

Ernie stopped the saw so they could hear each other. "Not long," James said. He never stayed long. Looking up at his son's awkward work, Ernie saw what James had inherited: wrapped tight to himself, his fine mouth slack-ened by unmet promise, James was the man Ernie might have been but for the steady love of a good woman.

"If you're still here on Friday, you can come watch the class," Francine said, then turned for home.

James flashed that smile again—Marie, Marie—and called after her, "I don't think I'm ready to see my father in tap shoes."

"You'd be surprised what a man is ready for," Ernie said.

"They're just regular shoes," Francine insisted, her voice sailing over the gate. "You don't get taps unless you want them."

"Right-o," James said, chuckling a little—a pleasant, foreign sound, easy on the ears. Ernie dug into the work, feeling good, a flimsy breeze easing across his shoulders.

The remains of the afternoon felt reminiscent of the first time he'd been up here, hammering and nailing and showing off for his wife. He cleared out some debris from the biggest gaps, leaving alone the ones that looked like active nests. Car horns sounded here and there throughout the afternoon. "What's all that?" James asked. He had his sleeves rolled up, his forearms, though not strong, looking a lot like his father's.

"Victory," Ernie said. He started to tell James the story of the town's long, unhappy road to working again, but as it turned out, there was too much of it he didn't know, and so his story was short, not much more detailed than what he'd read in the papers. He would have to get out, ask around, get the lay of the land again.

"Dad," James said, wiping his forehead, "there's standing water all over this thing. Shouldn't we be waterproofing the wood or something?"

"That's a loser's game, son," Ernie said. "There's no staying ahead of it."

"It's going to rot away eventually."

"I imagine so," Ernie said. "But there's nothing wrong with looking handsome in the meanwhile."

James shrugged. "Suit yourself," he said, patting the ark's broad side. Above them the afternoon sky floated smooth and blue as a tablecloth. *Ping*, went their hammers. *Ping*, went their nails. They worked long into evening, father and son, battening down the hatches, two by two.

Coming Home
to Abbott Falls

An Afterword

For the past thirty years—at readings, signings, book club meetings, and other festive occasions—readers have been asking me about the writing life. I'm grateful for these questions, and surprised that people care enough to ask at all. As for the answers, it depends on who's asking, which book is in process, and how well the work is going on the given day. I often wind up on oratorial detours and roundabouts, for the writing biz is a gambler's game, mysterious and dysfunctional, packed with suspense and full-circles and paradox. Sometimes I'm compelled to give contradictory answers to the same query. (*"I love writing. Thanks for asking. Also, I hate writing."*)

Only one question—*"Which book is your personal favorite?"*—gets the same simple answer: *Ernie's Ark*. Every time. Without caveat.

Ernie's Ark, first published in 2002, is the book that laid the groundwork for both my memoir, *When We Were the Kennedys*, and my first play, *Papermaker*. It starred as the "community read" in places I might not have visited otherwise, and introduced me to readers who surprised the heck out of me, like the bewhiskered woodsman who said that until *Ernie's Ark* he hadn't read a book since high school. The book gave rise to makeshift arks ornamenting library dooryards, and to theatrical readings on mainstages and in grange halls. I loved this book for its eccentric reach, and because it gave me so much more than I ever expected.

A few years ago, however, I began to meet readers who had never heard of my "personal favorite." *Ernie's Ark* had suddenly become difficult to find. Used copies turned up hither and yon—some lovingly dogeared, others pristinely unread—but the book slipped out of print and no reliable source remained. I heard regularly from booksellers, teachers, and book clubs asking if I had copies to sell. How dismaying, to say the least, to know that a book so embraced by readers, and a book I remembered with such affection, had begun to vanish from the literary universe. When Joshua Bodwell, editorial director at David R. Godine, asked if he could help resurrect *Ernie's Ark* in a new edition, I jumped at the chance.

I am an inveterate reviser. I revise all the way through editing, copyediting, typesetting, and beyond. More than once I've tried the patience of a production editor with the subject line: ONE MORE CHANGE? Once a book goes off to the printer, though, it's over: I let go, and that's that.

So, you can imagine my glee, given a fresh chance to revisit a book I'd long ago put to bed. The author of *Ernie's Ark* was younger and less seasoned than I; here was my chance to correct her inexperience. Of course, I grasped that the younger me had known loss, that she had the chops to describe the wallop of grief that accompanies a labor strike. But I had eighteen years on her now, and life had continued to school me. How might I alter Ernie and Marie's story of love through illness, having since felt the shock of illness inside my own marriage? How might I rethink Dan Little's response to his vanishing brother, having since held my own sister's hand as she died? Life brings us to our knees, yes it does, and for a writer, the aftermath of a great humbling cannot help but change the work.

Red pencil at the ready, I opened *Ernie's Ark* intending to hunt down every hiccup, to cut and add and cut again, to polish my poor book until you could barely see it for the shine. Quite the trick, and wholly unnecessary, because once I began reading I was so glad to be in Abbott Falls again. The characters hailed from my home tribe—a papermill town in western Maine—the first of my books to do so. Here was Francine, my young striver; and Ernie, my old striver; and Henry John McCoy, the titan of industry who can't fathom his own daughter; and Kenny Love, living his dead uncle's life; and all the other angry, befuddled, righteous, decent souls who cross each other's paths throughout nine intertwined stories. Like friends of my youth, they reminded me where I came from.

They also reminded me where *they* came from. Rereading certain scenes, even certain lines, conjured moments of conception. The notion of a "happy scale" hit me as I stared out the window at my neighbor's snow-burdened spruce; Cindy Love's prowess at parlor games arrived as

I sipped a latte at Java Joe's in Portland, Maine. Both the tree and the coffee shop are gone; the book remains.

Ernie's Ark is the only book I didn't have to write and rewrite a hundred times, because the characters arrived mercifully whole. And, in piercing contrast to my other books, *Ernie's Ark* gave me not one moment of writerly despair. In fact, it's the only book I've enjoyed writing all the way through; I'm talking unmitigated delight, at every stage, start to finish. For that alone, I altered nary a syllable.

Before its original publication, *Ernie's Ark* contained ten stories in manuscript. My editor at the time—the incomparable Jay Schaefer at Chronicle Books—thought that "Hush, Little Baby" did not belong to the whole. It's the one story that takes place outside of Abbott Falls, and its cooler prose lends an odd counterpoint to the warm timbre of the other stories. But Josh insisted that my readers would embrace the full sweep of the original manuscript, so here I am, persuaded by a current editor to include a story that a former editor urged me to dis-include. (See above, under: *Readers' questions, the writing biz, full circle.*)

I look upon my older work the way I look upon my past in general, with as much love and forgiveness as I can muster. It's a good way to live a writing life. And so, with deep thanks to Josh and the team at David R. Godine, I welcome *Ernie's Ark* back into the world. I wish it well, and hope you will too.

—Monica Wood
Maine, 2020

ACKNOWLEDGMENTS

First and always, immense thanks to Dan Abbott, who lives every page of every book with me. Thanks also to Gail Hochman, my literary north star; no writer could ask for more love and loyalty, and I return it tenfold. Marianne Merola, too, sparkles in that universe. Thanks to Josh Bodwell and his impressive team at David R. Godine, for bringing Ernie and the gang back into the world in brand-new clothes. I'm so delighted and grateful. Jay Schaefer was the original editor for this book and I remain thankful for his skill and wisdom.

Although Abbott Falls is a composite of paper-mill towns and cities all over the country, I owe a special debt to my hometown of Mexico, Maine, and to the old friends and neighbors who remain close to my heart. I also thank my brother, Barry, whose life and work influenced parts of this book.

Some of these stories have previously appeared in print: "Ernie's Ark" in *Glimmer Train Stories* and the *Pushcart*

Prize Anthology 1999; "That One Autumn" in *Glimmer Train Stories;* "Take Care Good Boy" in *Yankee;* "The Temperature of Desire" in *Orchid;* and "At the Mercy" (under a different title) in *Confrontation.* My sincere thanks to the editors of these publications.

ABOUT THE AUTHOR

MONICA WOOD is a novelist, memoirist, and play-wright. In 2019 she received the Maine Humanities Council Carlson Prize for contributions to the public humanities, and in 2018 received the Maine Writers & Publishers Alliance Distinguished Achievement Award for contributions to the literary arts.

Wood's most recent novel, *The One-in-a-Million Boy*, has been translated into twenty languages. She is also the author of the memoir *When We Were the Kennedys*, a New England bestseller, summer-reading pick in *O, The Oprah Magazine*, and winner of the May Sarton Memoir Award and the Maine Literary Award. Her novel *Any Bitter Thing* was an ABA bestseller and Book Sense Top Ten pick. Her other fiction includes *Ernie's Ark*, which has been excerpted on NPR's "Selected Shorts" and se-lected by several towns and cities as their "One Book, One Community" read; *My Only Story*, a finalist for the Kate Chopin Award; and *Secret Language*, her first novel.

Her widely anthologized short stories have won a Pushcart Prize and been featured on public radio. Her nonfiction has appeared in *O, The Oprah Magazine, New York Times, Martha Stewart Living, Parade*, and many other publications.

In 2015 Wood's first play, *Papermaker,* debuted in an extended run at Portland Stage in Portland, Maine, and quickly set the theater's all-time attendance record. Her second play, *The Half-Light*, debuted at Portland Stage in 2019 and became the theater's second bestselling show ever.

A NOTE ON THE TYPE

This book is set in Caslon. Our modern version is based upon the early 18th century roman types of William Caslon I, the first independent British printer. His great contributions were also warmly received in America. His type was employed for setting the Declaration of Independence. The Caslon family's foundry continued under their own name until 1937.

Book Design by Brooke Koven

1970–2020
David R. Godine
Publisher
FIFTY YEARS